Vivian was the youngest of the troupe, barely sixteen.

With her thin frame, Vivian was a natural to play parts that required a woman to pose as a man. From what gossip Reggie had overheard, Vivian had a somewhat less than virtuous background. She had already made none-too-subtle suggestions to Reggie which let him know she would not be averse to his attentions. Unfortunately for Vivian, Reggie's attentions were not drawn to the ladies.

Now Vivian's pinched expression made her look far younger than her sixteen years. "Please, no," she said. She shrank back in her seat, as far away from the bandit as she could get.

Reggie wasn't sure what possessed him. "Don't," he said. "Wait. I have something..."

Comstock

AARON MICHAELS

ᴛVᴘ

Thunder Valley Press

Comstock

AARON MICHAELS

CHAPTER ONE

1883

Waking up to find a pistol pointed at him was not the way Reginald Grayson expected his career as a serious actor to begin. He wasn't even at his destination yet, only on a stagecoach en route to Virginia City along with the three other principal members of the San Francisco Shakespeare Company.

"That's it," came the muffled voice of the bandit holding the pistol. "Empty your pockets, kind sir, now that you've rejoined the waking."

The man had no face. Or, more precisely, no face Reggie could see. A hood covered the bandit's head. The only features visible were shadowy blue eyes staring at Reggie through two small holes cut in the rough burlap. The bandit's voice was strangely accented, but all Reggie could focus on was the cold metal barrel of the pistol.

"I'm a poor actor," Reggie said. "I have nothing worth stealing." Which was almost the truth.

The bandit made no reply except to gesture with the pistol and tilt his head in such a way that Reggie understood he would judge for himself whether anything Reggie carried was worth thieving.

Reggie knew better than to expect help from the other man in the coach. Reggie might sleep during interminable coach journeys, but it appeared Jeremiah Sommersby found relief from boredom in a cheap bottle of whiskey. Currently the esteemed Mr. Sommersby was passed out, propped up on his seat next to Reggie, the remains of his latest bottle clutched loosely in his well-manicured hand.

The two actresses in the coach were no better. Well-bred ladies, they were, Vivian and Blanche had told Reggie when he was hired as an understudy eight months ago. Apparently ladies did not raise a hand against a criminal except in surrender. Which Blanche and Vivian were doing quite nicely at the moment.

The bandit leaned closer and used the pistol to nudge Reggie's coat open.

Reggie kept what money he had in a small leather pouch in his trouser pocket. What he kept in the inside pocket of his coat was much more valuable, but only to him, and he had no intention of giving it up.

"Don't make me search you," the bandit said in his strange accent. "It would not be pleasant... for you."

The man sounded like he might be smiling behind his hood. Reggie found being robbed unpleasant enough. He had no wish to be handled by the man in a search for valuables.

"Very well," Reggie said, trying to project a confidence and worldly calm he did not feel. "If you'll let me reach into my pocket..."

The bandit nodded and lifted the pistol

away from Reggie's coat. "Only your purse," the bandit said. "It would not be wise to reach for your own pistol."

That wouldn't be a problem. Reggie didn't own a gun. He'd never fired one in his entire life, and even if he had, he wouldn't have been so foolish as to reach for it now.

Reggie removed the small leather pouch from his trousers. The bandit took it in his gloved hand and put it in his own pocket.

"Now, for the ladies," the bandit said.

"We don't have anything!" Blanche's voice held a timid quaver, so different from the confident tone she projected on stage. Reggie couldn't tell if she was acting, or if she was indeed terrified for her life.

The bandit nudged the silver chain Blanche wore around her neck. Suspended from the chain was a small vial Blanche claimed contained holy water blessed by her parish priest, which she carried for good luck. Reggie suspected the vial contained something vastly different from holy water.

"Sir!" Blanche wasn't acting now; she was truly affronted and genuinely frightened. Of the bandit or of losing her "good luck," Reggie couldn't tell.

The bandit seemed to reconsider. "You have nothing... else... of value?"

Blanche searched through the voluminous folds of her dress and pulled out a small beaded purse from a hidden pocket. "It's all I have. If you take it, you'll leave me penniless."

"But not without recourse," the bandit said. He took the purse from Blanche's trembling fingers and put it in the same pocket where he'd placed Reggie's pouch. "And you, young miss?"

Vivian was the youngest of the troupe, barely sixteen.

With her thin frame, Vivian was a natural to play parts that required a woman to pose as a man. From what gossip Reggie had overheard, Vivian had a somewhat less than virtuous background. She had already made none-too-subtle suggestions to Reggie which let him know she would not be averse to his attentions. Unfortunately for Vivian, Reggie's attentions were not drawn to the ladies.

Now Vivian's pinched expression made her

look far younger than her sixteen years. "Please, no," she said. She shrank back in her seat, as far away from the bandit as she could get.

Reggie wasn't sure what possessed him. "Don't," he said. "Wait. I have something..."

The bandit turned his attention—and his pistol—back to Reggie. His eyes held a look of surprise. "You wish me to leave the young lady be. What do you have left to offer me?"

Reggie removed his father's watch from his coat pocket. The watch was the sole legacy the senior Mr. Grayson had left his only son before sailing from London for fame and fortune. Reggie had never seen him again.

The watch was silver; an ornately-worked scene of London Bridge on the case protected the polished crystal inside. The crystal had a small chip from when Reggie had dropped the watch as a child. His father's name—Simon E. Grayson—was engraved inside the cover in flowing script.

The watch had no real value to anyone except Reggie, but the bandit took it anyway when Reggie held it toward him.

The money had been easier to hand over

than the watch. Money Reggie could always earn; the watch was irreplaceable.

Reggie swallowed hard as the bandit slipped the watch inside his coat as well. Reggie tried to tell himself that the watch was merely an item and worth far less than his life. He almost believed it.

"A fair trade, sir," the bandit said. He withdrew from the coach with a nod of his head and a small bow.

A bandit with manners. Reggie was surprised.

"Do not follow me," the bandit said, his voice harder now. "And do not attempt to leave the coach until you count to one hundred. If you open the door sooner, I'll know, and it will not go well for you."

The bandit shut the door against the frightened actors. A moment later Reggie heard the bandit's horse gallop away. He did not hear any other horses follow.

The entire company of actors had been robbed by a single man wearing a hood and brandishing a pistol.

Reggie didn't know whether to be embarrassed that the company had allowed itself to be robbed in such a manner, or impressed with the bandit for his sheer audacity in attacking a coach guarded not only by the driver but by a second man as well. Reggie had assumed the additional man was necessary to spell the driver during the long journey, but perhaps the bandit had robbed other travelers on this road.

In the end, it didn't matter. The result was the same. Reggie would arrive in Virginia City, one of the richest mining towns in the West, penniless and without the only thing his father had left for him.

Blanche called for the stagecoach driver. A soft moan came from the ground outside the coach. Reggie hoped the men had not been badly injured. He had never driven a coach, and Jeremiah was too drunk to keep himself seated upright inside, much less outside in the driver's seat.

Vivian was looking at him with an odd expression on her face. "Why did you do that?" she asked. "You owe me nothing."

Reggie ignored her and slumped in his own seat. If he couldn't explain his motivations to himself, he certainly couldn't explain them to her.

He wished for some of Jeremiah's whisky. A lot of Jeremiah's whiskey. He'd been excited at the beginning of this trip. He would finally be on stage, and not just as an understudy, but as an actor. Now he felt hollow. He just wanted to go back to San Francisco, where men were civilized.

This was not what he expected. Not at all.

CHAPTER TWO

Piper's Opera House wasn't what Reggie expected either.

Granted, Virginia City was a much rougher town than San Francisco. Reggie supposed any theater in such a place would tend to reflect the nature of the audience it served.

The opera house did have all the things Reggie had become familiar with in his years as an understudy for various companies: a stage lit by a semi-circle of small lanterns along the front edge in black-painted holders which re- flected light on the actors and none on the audience; private boxes set high above both sides of the stage, complete with high-backed, heavy seats and gilt-edged velvet curtains; rough-hewn pine flooring covered with scuff marks and stains which didn't bear close examination. But Reggie had certainly had never imagined he would be performing in a theater attached to the rear of a raucous saloon filled with drunken miners and half-naked whores.

How could he possibly perform Shakespeare in a setting like this? Shakespeare's words were meant to be performed with nuance and subtle shifts of tone, not shouted in order to compete with the drunken revelry of the saloon.

The jangling tunes of the saloon's honky-tonk piano jarred Reggie's nerves. He hoped the piano player would refrain from playing during the company's performance.

The piano was out of tune, and the clash of sound was driving Reggie to distraction. During rehearsal he'd already missed so many of his lines, he felt like the worst of understudies. He finally had to excuse himself from the stage, claiming a headache.

He sat alone in his dressing room—his very

own dressing room—and held his head in his hands. He'd thought performing in a frontier town would be an adventure. He'd read stories about Virginia City, dime novels that made the boomtown seem like such an exciting place to be, but he'd never imagined the reality of a town that existed solely due to the vast silver mines in its midst.

He'd read all about the tunnels that honey-combed through the ground hundreds of feet below the city, a maze of passages held in place by thick timbers and determination. In the few days the company had been in Virginia City, Reggie had gone exploring when he wasn't re-hearsing. He'd seen miners newly emerged from the tunnels, their faces so black with dirt that their eyes, ghostly white, were the only things that differentiated one man from the next.

And he'd seen the men who owned the mines, important in their new suits and hats and freshly-minted wealth. Perhaps those men, the owners, would be the ones to see him perform. The miners looked too weary. The ones who drank in the saloon certainly looked barely able to lift a glass to their lips, much less understand the beauty of Shakespeare's language.

Reggie looked at his reflection in the mirror. Lamplight made his features soft, his eyes dark.

"I need this job," he told himself.

The hotel had extended credit to the actors, confident their lodging would be paid for from the proceeds of the performances. Reggie had no other means to pay his way. He didn't fancy ending up playing piano in a saloon or tending bar. He was meant to be an actor. He just hadn't shown it on stage today, and the company's first performance was that night. At this rate, a trained horse would do better.

A soft knock at his door roused Reggie from his thoughts.

"Mr. Grayson?"

Reggie didn't recognize the voice. "Yes?" he asked.

"I've a delivery for Mr. Reginald Grayson. Are you he, sir?"

Reggie opened the door. A boy, no more than twelve, stood outside. His clothes were covered with a fine layer of dust, his shoes mud-caked, but his face and hands were clean.

He held an envelope in his hands.

"I'm Reggie Grayson."

The boy handed him the envelope. "This is yours, sir."

Reggie took the envelope. He had no coin to give the boy for his troubles.

Reggie looked at his dressing table. "Wait," he told the boy. He had a spare leather thong he used to tie his hair back when he was on stage. He handed it to the boy, whose own hair hung loose around his face. "It's the best I have," he said in apology. "I wish it was more."

The boy took it with wide eyes. "Thank you, sir."

The boy folded the strip of leather and put it in his pocket like it was made of gold. Or perhaps, in Virginia City, it would have been made of silver.

"Good luck to you, sir," the boy said.

He ran down the narrow hallway before Reggie could ask who sent him. Perhaps the answer was in the envelope.

Reggie shut his door and turned his attention his delivery. The envelope bore no markings on the outside save his own name.

He broke the seal. Inside the envelope he found a single sheet of paper. He unfolded it and gasped.

It was a drawing of himself on stage. And not on just any stage—on this stage. In the drawing, Reggie was dressed in the clothes he'd worn the day before during rehearsal.

No one in the company had drawn this, Reggie was sure of it. Jeremiah was an adequate actor, but he had no ability with pen and ink. Reggie couldn't imagine either Vivian or Blanche drawing this either, and only Vivian still had money to pay a messenger. Jeremiah had been robbed on the stage while he slept off the whiskey, and he was as penniless as Reggie.

Griffin DuMont, the company's manager, had no creative ability beyond his skill at obtaining work for his actors. While the company employed artists who designed elaborate sets for the performances in San Francisco, when the company toured, the actors made do with whatever was available.

No artists had traveled with the actors to Virginia City, and the few assistants DuMont needed to haul the heavy trunks of costumes and small props, he hired locally. The rehearsals had not been open to the public, although Reggie imagined someone could have watched from the back door of the saloon. Or from the shadowy private boxes.

Reggie took the drawing to his dressing table. He compared his image in the mirror to the image of himself on paper.

The artist was talented—more than talented, if Reggie was fair. The drawing captured the subtle change in Reggie's natural posture when he let the character transform him from a simple penniless young actor into an aristocratic young lord in love with a woman disguised as a man in Shakespeare's *Twelfth Night*. His eyes on the page held the same sparkle as his eyes did now in the reflected lamplight.

Whoever had drawn this had spent time studying him and had drawn it with as much feeling as Reggie put into his performances. But who? It would have taken time to get to know him like this, and no one here had had time to get to know him.

Reggie looked inside the envelope, studied the outside of the envelope, the reverse side of the drawing, hoping for a clue, but none appeared. He refolded the drawing and placed it back in the envelope.

Jeremiah had told him about people—women and men both—who developed an unhealthy obsession with actors. Reggie had known some of what Jeremiah said was mere wishful thinking on Jeremiah's part. No one had obsessed about Jeremiah in years, if Blanche was to be believed.

Did Reggie have his first admirer? Someone who was impressed with him for what he did, not who he was?

No, he didn't think so. At least not in the way Jeremiah meant it. This person, whoever she—or he—was, was a talented artist in their own right. The drawing was a gift, and Reggie would treat it as such.

His first gift, for his first role.

He tucked the envelope with the drawing in the pocket of his coat. It made him feel somewhat better, knowing someone out there admired him. Perhaps he would be able to get through tonight's performance without incident after all. Positive thinking, and all that.

He just wished he knew who to thank for the drawing.

CHAPTER THREE

Reggie would not soon forget his first performance of Shakespeare's *Twelfth Night*.

The audience in Piper's Opera house had been a strange mixture of the upper class of Virginia City society—well-dressed and refined in their response to the play—and drunken men who seemed to think the play needed their active participation.

Jeremiah had to improvise at one point to prevent a drunken man who'd climbed on stage from kissing Vivian, even though she was in her male disguise. The audiences in San Francisco had never behaved so.

Reggie stuck to his rehearsed performance as much as possible, but the reaction of the audience had distracted him. Even when relatively well-behaved, the audience's unpredictability made Reggie tense, and his performance felt stiff and unnatural.

As bad as that had been, it was nowhere near as disastrous as when the company's director had introduced him to Beatrice Weatherly at a small reception following the evening's performance.

Mrs. Weatherly was a patron of the arts, or so the company's director had been told. A matronly woman with a kind face and rotund waist—someone Reggie thought was the quintessential grandmotherly type—she had taken one look at Reggie, become white as a ghost, and promptly fainted at his feet.

"It's your face, you see," said Mr. Weatherly, a thin, rather pale-faced man with a mustache so bushy and untamed it looked like someone had pasted a squirrel's tail on his upper lip. "You bear a striking resemblance to Grover Mackey, young man."

"Grover Mackey?" The name had no meaning for Reggie.

"Mr. Mackey passed on," Mr. Weatherly said. He looked uncomfortable even discussing the subject. "Some years past. He was a fine young man, the son of John Mackey, was he. It's likely that's what gave my wife the vapors."

Mr. Weatherly crouched at his wife's side and patted her hand. Her eyes fluttered open.

"That's it, my dear," Mr. Weatherly said. "See, 'tis just the actor who entertained us so well this evening, not young Mackey come back from the grave."

Reggie had never been told he resembled a dead man before. He found the idea disquieting, to say the least.

"How did he pass on?" he asked.

A small crowd of people stood knotted around the fallen Mrs. Weatherly. "Drowned, I heard," one of them said. "In the mines."

How could a person drown in the mines? Unless there was—

"Wasn't no drowning," said another man. "I heard it was the elevator down there, lopped his head clean off." The man pantomimed his words with a finger drawn across the side of his neck. "Some say he was pushed out as the car went down, caught his head on a timber."

"Sir!"

The protest came from Mr. Weatherly, who'd gone back to tending his wife. She had apparently fainted again at the thought of poor Grover Mackey losing his life in such a gruesome fashion.

Reggie wasn't fond of the idea either. He had to keep himself from rubbing the back of his own neck just to make sure his head was still attached.

"Wasn't any of that," said another man. "Just a simple cave-in. Crushed beneath rocks and timber. That's the chance he took, just like all them others, working in the mines."

Mrs. Weatherly didn't appear to be waking up any time soon.

"I'm sorry to have upset your wife so," Reggie said to Mr. Weatherly. "Perhaps I should—"

He glanced around for some way out of the conversation. Across the room, he saw a thin, sandy-haired man watching him, and not in what appeared to be a casual way.

Reggie felt a reaction within himself that he hadn't felt in a long time, almost as if he and this man had some connection.

Was this man his secret artist?

When the man's eyes met Reggie's, he looked away, as if he didn't want to be caught staring.

Even if he wasn't the man who had left the drawing, Reggie wanted to meet him, hear his voice, look into his eyes and maybe touch—

"I should meet some of the other patrons," Reggie said before he allowed himself to finish that thought. He bowed his head toward Mr. and Mrs. Weatherly. "I'm pleased to meet you both," he said, even though it was clear only Mr. Weatherly could hear him.

Reggie left the knot of people before the poor woman could wake up and he unwittingly upset her again. He received well wishes and congratulations as he crossed the room. Apparently his performance hadn't been so lacking from the audience's perspective.

He didn't stop to talk to anyone, but still, by the time he'd reached the spot where the thin man had been standing, the man was gone.

Reggie tried not to feel disappointed. The fact that the man had been watching didn't mean anything. Everyone watched actors, or so Jeremiah had told him.

"No matter what fine clothes you wear, their eyes will strip you to your skin," Jeremiah had said one night when he'd had enough whiskey and wanted someone to talk to. "Eventually you'll learn to like it."

Alone again with his thoughts, Reggie allowed himself to feel a small thrill at the idea of this man stripping him to his skin. The man had been thin, true, but his clean-shaven face had been handsome, with high, chiseled cheekbones and a dimpled chin. He had striking eyes beneath shoulder-length, sandy-brown hair. Reggie wondered if he was a miner. Many of the miners he'd seen were rail-thin, although this man wasn't as pale as most. He'd been dressed well, but not overly so, as the wealthy men in the room seemed to be.

Reggie wandered the room from group to group, but he couldn't find the one man he wanted to find. He left as soon as it was polite to do so and retired to his dressing room, where he found another surprise waiting for him.

There, in the middle of his dressing room table, unaccompanied by note or other explanation, was his father's watch.

CHAPTER FOUR

The San Francisco Shakespeare Company had arranged rooms for the actors at the International Hotel.

At six stories tall and with a working elevator, the hotel boasted that it was the finest in the land between Chicago and San Francisco. Reggie didn't know about that, but with a sturdy four-poster bed covered with fine linens, ornately carved wainscoting, and a panoramic view of the city, his room was certainly the finest in which Reggie had ever found himself.

He placed his father's watch on the table

next to the bed before he changed into his nightclothes.

Why had the watch been returned to him? And by whom? The bandit?

Had the thief been to tonight's performance?

Reggie slipped between icy sheets. The nights were cold here in Virginia City, even though it was late spring and the days were warm.

He drew the covers up to his neck, shivering at the memory of a pistol pointed at him and shadowed, blue eyes staring at him through slits in a burlap mask.

He'd turned the room's oil lamp down low; the dim light left most of his room in shadows. From outside his window, he could hear the raucous sounds of night life in Virginia City.

The town had more saloons than Reggie had ever seen. Saloons and gambling halls and whorehouses, and most of them seemed to be open all hours of the day and night.

At the party tonight, he'd been invited more than once to accompany someone to a saloon, but he had declined each invitation. None had come from the sandy-haired man he'd seen watching him, but from businessmen who apparently lived under the delusion that actors were wealthy men with substantial money to invest in their businesses.

It seemed yet another man had watched him tonight—the bandit who had robbed the stagecoach. The man had kept Reggie's money, but returned the watch. He'd shown compassion, of a sort—the same compassion he'd shown Vivian?

Reggie didn't know what to make of that. He wasn't helpless, even though the robbery had certainly made him feel helpless at the time.

Without warning, the bed beneath Reggie shuddered. He heard a dull *whomp,* and the light seemed to shiver as the glass lamp rattled against the table.

An earthquake? Reggie had felt earthquakes in San Francisco. Unsettling, knowing the earth wasn't as solid as it appeared. But this wasn't an earthquake. He heard shouts in the street and then the clanging of an alarm.

Reggie rushed to the window. The ever-present smoke that hung over the city from the smokestacks of the Orphir mine, the closest of several large mines scattered throughout the town itself, seemed like a shroud. Reggie could see no fire or flames, just a cloud of dust over the Orphir rising up to meet the smoke, and he shivered anew as he realized what must have happened.

One of the tunnels beneath the city had caved in. He wondered how many men were trapped below ground.

How many had died.

He watched at the window for a long time as mine workers responded to the cave in. What must it be like to work in a mine? He had never been claustrophobic, but he didn't think he could spend long hours so deep beneath the earth with the constant danger that the ground above him might fall and crush him at any moment. No wonder the miners drank so heavily. Perhaps they needed to numb themselves in order to do their jobs.

The annoyance he'd felt earlier with his performance seemed less important somehow. Acting was not life and death, but merely entertainment.

"Middle of the night thoughts," he murmured to himself.

It was something his mum was fond of saying when Reggie sometimes found her sitting alone in a rocking chair late at night. She had done that often after his father left.

Perhaps she did that now that he was gone as well. He'd wanted to bring her with him to America, but she hadn't wanted to leave her home.

He wrote her when he could and thought of her often. He missed her desperately at times. He had resigned himself to being alone, but that didn't mean he enjoyed his loneliness. His need for companionship made him turn a simple glance from a stranger into something that could mean more, just as it made him think the gift of a drawing meant more than it did.

"Ridiculous," he muttered.

Actors were an imaginative sort, but really, he shouldn't let his imaginings get the better of him. It would lead to nothing, and Reggie would still be alone. Whores were plentiful in places like Virginia City for men with coin, but a man who preferred the company of another man needed to be careful. Becoming enamored of a stranger for no reason other than polite interest was dangerous.

He turned to go back to his bed when a glimpse of something beneath his door caught his attention.

Reggie frowned. Whatever it was, hadn't been there before, he would swear it.

He brought the oil lamp from his bedside table to the door. There, on the dark-patterned carpet, was another envelope like the one the messenger boy had delivered.

He picked the envelope up with trembling fingers. He didn't wait to take it back to his bed, but ripped the envelope open where he stood by the door.

Inside was another drawing of him, this one from the party that evening.

In the drawing, he was conversing with the company's director, whose figure was sketched in only lightly. Reggie, however, was drawn with infinite care. The artist had caught the tilt of Reggie's head, the slight curve of his lips, and most importantly, the yearning look in his eyes as he searched the room for a glimpse of the thin man who had been watching him.

Like a sleepwalker, Reggie took the first drawing from the pocket of his coat. He unfolded it and put both drawings side by side on the table.

The rough paper was the same. The artist's style was the same. Clearly, he had an admirer. But why wouldn't the man come forward?

Maybe he had, in the only way he knew how. As careful as Reggie had to be, perhaps this man—through station or circumstance—had to be even more careful in approaching Reggie.

If anything was to come of this, Reggie would have to first discover who his admirer was, and then decide what, if anything, to do about it.

Reggie found himself hoping that the mysterious artist and the thin, sandy-haired man were one and the same. He didn't want to think about what would happen if the artist turned out to be the bandit who'd returned his watch, or what would happen if the men—two, or were there three?—who seemed to have taken an interest in him found out about each other.

CHAPTER FIVE

The cave in at the Orphir mine was the talk of the hotel the next morning when Reggie went down to breakfast.

Reggie sat by himself at a small corner table as had become his habit since the acting company had arrived at the hotel. Jeremiah Sommersby never ate breakfast—perhaps he drank it instead in the privacy of his room. Blanche and Vivian preferred to sleep late and ate together after Reggie had already left to explore the city during his daily walk from the hotel to the opera house.

As an actor, Reggie was a natural eaves-dropper. He studied people, their habits and their words, to use in his portrayals of various characters. He had learned to sit by himself with a newspaper open in front of him and pretend to read while really paying attention to the people around him. A newspaper as a prop made him part of the background, and he'd found most people would ignore him and discuss things freely as if he wasn't there at all.

This morning what the people around him were talking about were the men who had died the night before in the mine.

"Tragedy," said a middle-aged man in a fine tailored suit two tables away from Reggie. A silver-handled walking stick was propped against his chair.

The man's companion was a thin young woman who wore her auburn hair pulled pain-fully tight into a bun at the nape of her neck. She dabbed at her pale lips with a napkin, her eyes downcast. Her dress was plain but well-made, the color a dusty brown. She paid more attention to a boy of about six who sat quietly at the table with the two adults. Reggie wondered

if she was the man's wife, or perhaps a gover-
ness for the child.

"Tragedy," the man said again. "William's
been cautioned about pushing his men too
hard." He used a biscuit to sop up the gravy on
his plate. "Tired men make mistakes."

The woman in brown said nothing, but the
skin around her eyes had a pinched look. Reggie wondered if she knew any of the miners
who had died.

Two other men, bankers possibly by the cut
of their clothes and their self-important stride
through the dining hall, stopped by the table to
talk to the man with the walking stick.

"We're going to have to do something
about this, Joseph," said the first of the two, a
man who clearly did not miss many meals
judging by the size of his rotund belly. "Cummings won't listen to reason, sending men
down that deep without proper—"

"Hush," said the man with the cane as he
glanced around the room, presumably to see
who might have overheard.

Reggie focused his attention on his meal.
He might not be able to watch them, but listen-

ing was just as good.

"You know what we mean," the second banker said, his voice little more than a stage whisper. Reggie was very good at hearing stage whispers.

The man with the cane glared at the two bankers. He was a fierce-looking man, and his glare silenced them both as effectively as a shout.

"No more talk of this here," the man named Joseph said.

Reggie glanced up again just in time to see the young woman flinch. Perhaps Joseph did more than speak harshly when he was annoyed.

"The men are dead. There's nothing to be done about it." Joseph looked at his silver-handled cane, then glanced at the woman. "It's a tragedy."

Only the tone of his voice didn't match his words. This man, whoever he was, cared less for the miners who died than he did the eggs on his plate.

Joseph spared a glance in Reggie's direction. A shiver went down Reggie's spine. He concentrated on his food and tried to project a disinterested air. He didn't know if he was successful. He hoped so.

The food itself no longer held any appeal for Reggie. Men had died last night, men he might have seen in the saloon in the front of the opera house. The man with the cane didn't care.

Reggie hadn't done anything to help last night, a fact he felt ashamed about in the cold light of morning. Now he felt an insane urge to do something, anything, to make this man understand that the lives of those dead men had mattered. He wished he had the courage to explain to this man that all men, rich and powerful or poor and needy, deserved to be mourned, but he didn't.

Instead he sat and pushed his food around his plate, just like he'd stayed in his room last night, only now he said his own silent prayers for the men—the strangers—who had died and the families they left behind.

CHAPTER SIX

Vivian and Blanche were waiting for Reggie in his dressing room when he finally made it to the opera house.

He'd spent a lot of time walking the streets of Virginia City. At first, he'd been concerned that someone might have followed him out of the hotel, but he decided it was just his imagination given the conversation he'd overheard.

That worry removed, Reggie had turned his thoughts to the men in the mines, and more importantly, the type of man who would do what the three men at the table had insinuated—deliberately put men's lives in danger just to turn a bigger profit.

By the time he arrived at the opera house, it was almost time for the evening's first performance.

Vivian giggled when she saw Reggie.

He raised an eyebrow. "Do I have something on my face?"

He rubbed at his cheek. He'd been walking through the dusty town for some time. It was entirely possible he'd gotten himself dirty without realizing it.

Blanche leaned against his dressing table. Reggie could tell by her half-lidded gaze that she'd already sampled from her vial of good luck.

"You have a secret admirer," she said.

Reggie's breath caught in his throat. "What?"

She stepped away from the table, and Vivian giggled again.

There, in the middle of Reggie's dressing table, was a single red rose.

"Cheeky lady," Vivian said. "Sneaking in here and leaving that for you."

Reggie could feel the blush staining his face.

"Or is it?" Blanche asked.

Oh no. She couldn't mean...

She smiled at him. "Don't worry, dear Mr. Grayson." She touched his shoulder as she walked past him. Her hand felt limp and unpleasant. "We each have our admirers here. I'm sure yours is as well-intentioned—and appropriate—as ours."

Blanche took Vivian by the hand, and both ladies left his dressing room.

Reggie shut the door behind them and was dismayed to see his hand was trembling. So far, he had managed to keep his preferences a secret from everyone in the company.

He had lived a mostly solitary life in San Francisco, preferring to concentrate on his profession rather than seek out companionship, or even someone for just a means of release. He hadn't been with anyone in months.

Perhaps that was why he had allowed himself to daydream about the man—for he was sure it was a man—who had sent him the drawings, and about the thin, sandy-haired man from the night before.

But if Blanche suspected... Blanche was an addict, and addicts were unpredictable.

Reggie picked up the rose, careful of the thorns on the stem. The bud looked like it had come from someone's garden. The stem was short, the edge of the leaves brittle and brown.

He had seen few flowers here in his walks. Virginia City was a high mountain town; houses clung to the rocky slopes of Mount Davidson and crowded the narrow valley below. The air was thin. Not even pine trees grew on the craggy ground surrounding the city.

The gift of a rose here meant something.

"Who are you?" Reggie whispered. He traced the petals with a light touch, imagined someone touching his skin with the same kind of care. "I want to meet you. See you. I want..."

What he wanted he couldn't have.

He put the rose back on his dressing table and began to get ready for the evening's performance. At least on stage, if not in life, he could be someone who found love.

CHAPTER SEVEN

The first performance of the night went badly. Attendance was poor, the private boxes nearly empty, and those who did attend were subdued, unlike the patrons of the saloon. Reggie could hear them through the walls, loud and rowdy.

He had a hard time finding his character; Shakespeare's words felt dull and lifeless as he spoke them. He kept stealing glances at the audience, wondering if the person who'd left the rose was there.

At one point Reggie thought he saw the

thin, sandy-haired man in the darkened box to the left of the stage. Someone was there in the shadows, he could have sworn it, but when he had a chance to look again, the box was empty.

By the time the performance was over, Reggie was beyond frustrated.

He usually spent the time between performances in his dressing room. Tonight he couldn't stand to stay there, looking at that single rose.

He changed out of costume and went to the saloon instead.

The saloon was crowded, the air heavy with the smell of smoke and alcohol. Men stood at the bar and poured themselves whiskey as the bartender watched. Reggie counted three separate card games going at the tables as he walked through the saloon looking for an empty seat and a familiar face.

He finally found both at a table off to the side when he recognized the stagecoach driver. A whore had draped herself over the man's lap, but he waved Reggie over to his table anyway.

"Come, sit down," the driver said. He pushed a half-empty bottle of whiskey toward

Reggie. "Have a drink. You look like you could use one."

"Thank you."

Reggie picked up the bottle and hesitated only a moment before he took a long swallow. The whiskey burned his throat on the way down, but as it hit his belly, it seemed to take the edge off his emptiness.

He relaxed back against the chair.

"You look lonely, sitting there all by yourself," the whore said, her voice low with well-practiced sensuality. "I have a friend who'd be happy to keep you company."

"No. Thank you," Reggie said. "I have to go back on stage later, but I appreciate the offer," he added hastily, just in case his refusal had sounded too abrupt.

She shrugged and turned her attention back to the driver. "I have a room," she said. "Right across the street." She picked up the bottle Reggie had put back on the table. "We could take this bottle and go have a nice little time, just the two of us."

The driver rubbed his hand up and down her back. "I'd like to do that, Charlotte, I certainly would. But I'm afraid I can't afford you tonight, what with my pay docked 'n all."

Charlotte pouted—another well-practiced tool of her trade, Reggie was sure—and leaned forward to place a kiss on the driver's cheek. "Then I'll see you next time through, honey," she said, and she got up from the driver's lap to go find someone who could afford her company.

The driver watched her go with a sigh, then he took a long drink from the bottle.

"Your pay was docked?" Reggie asked.

The driver nodded.

"Because of what—the robbery?" Reggie thought of his father's watch, now safely back in his pocket.

"William fucking Cummings," the driver said. "He doesn't take it well when the stage I'm supposed to guard gets ambushed."

William Cummings. "The man who owns the Orphir mine owns the stagecoach, too?"

"One and the same," the driver said. "Tightwad bastard." The driver leaned forward. "His stages are the only ones robbed. When we transport goods, silver bars or all that fancy shit he and his missus fill their house with, we've got more guards than a fucking bank ever since he figured out that bastard only comes after us. But with you lot?" The driver's shoulders lifted in a shrug. "He sends just Jeb 'n me, and the two of us ain't never been enough against the cocksucker robbing us."

Reggie remembered the conversation he'd overheard that morning. It appeared a lot of people were not happy with Mr. Cummings, but to go so far as to rob his stagecoaches...

"Someone must have a vendetta against Mr. Cummings," Reggie said.

"Appears so, don't it?" The driver took another long drink from the bottle, then he leaned forward toward Reggie. "Look, I'm sorry we couldn't protect you. Bastard never hurts us, 'cept to knock us out with the butt end of that six shooter of his, so I guess I got that to be thankful for. Don't make no difference to you, though. He still stole from you, and for that I'm sorry."

The driver's alcohol and tobacco tinged breath drifted over the table toward Reggie, and he had to fight not to react to the sour smell.

"It wasn't your fault. As you say, no one was really hurt, and for that we should all be grateful."

That appeared to appease the driver's conscience. He nodded and offered the bottle to Reggie again, but Reggie shook his head. He couldn't afford to get drunk. He still had one more performance tonight.

"I should get back." Reggie stood up from the table and extended his hand to the driver. "I wish you the best on your next trip."

"That would be in three days' time." The driver smiled. "Got more passengers to transport, but I'm taking a little surprise for the cocksucker this time. Out of my own pocket, too, but I'm tired of getting robbed."

"A surprise?"

"Couple extra guards gonna trail along behind us," the driver said, his voice lowered so only Reggie could hear. "Gonna get rid of this problem once and for all."

The driver's smile got bigger, and it wasn't a pleasant sight.

Reggie's belly tightened around the whiskey. He couldn't get away from the table fast enough. He shoved his way through the crowded saloon, his thoughts on the bandit who'd robbed him of his money but then returned the one thing that meant more to Reggie than anything else he owned.

The driver clearly meant to ambush the bandit and kill him. Reggie found the idea more upsetting than he wanted to admit. And most upsetting of all was that he found himself wanting to warn the bandit, but he knew he couldn't. He didn't even know who the man was.

A solid ache settled in Reggie's heart as he made his way back to his dressing room.

He half expected to find something new on his dressing table, but the rose lay exactly where he'd left it, with no new drawing or other communication from his admirer.

When Reggie looked in the mirror, he imagined he saw shadowed, blue eyes looking back at him from behind a burlap mask.

"I'm sorry," Reggie murmured. "I wish..."

What did he wish?

He no longer had any idea.

CHAPTER EIGHT

The thin, sandy-haired man watched him again. Reggie was sure of it. He'd seen a rustle of movement in the back of the darkened box at the left of the stage, but the lantern light at the front of the stage had made it difficult to see anyone who might be hiding in the shadows.

Reggie had taken a chance. During one of his speeches, he'd played directly toward the box.

Vivian had reacted well and changed her own staging to accommodate him. Reggie was sure she would be angry with him later. He didn't care. He wanted to meet this man so badly, he felt like bounding off the stage and climbing up to the box just to reassure himself that the man was real.

He did exactly that as soon as the play was over and the actors had finished curtain call.

His instincts paid off.

He caught sight of the man leaving the theater through a private exit at the base of the stairs behind the box. Reggie hadn't even realized the exit was there.

"Wait!" Reggie called out.

The thin man turned, a look of shock on his handsome face, then he fled through the exit.

Reggie ran after him, heedless of the fact that the company's actors were forbidden to leave the theater while in costume.

"Please! I just want to meet you."

Reggie followed him into the darkened alleyway behind the theater.

The man ran through a series of narrow passageways and alleys behind the crowded businesses on the main street, deeper and deeper into the dark night. Reggie, for all his wanderings around Virginia City, quickly lost his sense of direction, but he doggedly kept going, getting just enough of a glimpse of the man running ahead of him to know he hadn't lost the man.

He had just rounded the corner of a brick building toward a deeply shadowed passageway when hands reached out of the darkness and grabbed him.

Reggie found himself shoved against the rough brick wall, the thin man's arms holding him still.

"Stop following me!" the man hissed in Reggie's face. "If I wanted to be seen by you, I would be."

They were both breathing hard from the chase. Unlike the driver's sour breath, the hint of tobacco on the thin man's breath smelled spicy and intriguing. His arms were hard, like metal bands.

Reggie didn't struggle against him, and in fact, found his body reacting to being held by this man in such a dark, secluded place.

"I wanted to meet you," Reggie said.

"I know what you want," the man said. "Such wants are dangerous in a place like this."

Reggie took a chance. "Then why have you

been sending me things? The drawings. And tonight, the rose."

He heard a hitch in the man's breath and knew he was right. This was the man who had drawn him in such exquisite, loving detail.

The man loosened his grip. "I shouldn't have done that." His voice lost the harsh edge and took on a melancholy tone. "I indulged myself. You reminded me..."

All of a sudden, it made sense. The red rose. It wasn't meant for him.

"I remind you of Grover Mackey," Reggie finished for him.

Reggie's eyes had become accustomed to the dark. He could see the outline of the man in front of him, and now Reggie saw the man nod.

A sharp pang of disappointment coursed through Reggie. The man had seen the same thing in him that Mrs. Weatherly had. The gifts weren't for him after all, but for a man who had died a tragic death.

"Was he..."

Reggie didn't finish the question. He didn't have to. As much as he knew this man had been watching him, he knew what this man and

Grover Mackey had been to each other.

"I'm sorry," Reggie said. "I should not have presumed that the gifts were meant for me. I merely–"

The kiss took Reggie by surprise.

The man's mouth was warm and insistent on his, and Reggie opened his own mouth without second thought.

He touched and tasted and was touched and tasted in return. His head swam with the unexpected intimacy of it, and he lost all sense of self and time. They could have been kissing for hours or mere moments. Reggie's legs felt weak, and he clutched at the man to hold himself upright.

When the man finally ended the kiss, Reggie was left gasping for breath, his body limp against the side of the building.

"The gifts were meant for you," the man said, his voice soft and raspy. "Only for you."

Reggie could feel the man's body trembling against him, and he believed what the man said. The disappointment he'd felt so sharply only moments before faded away.

"What is your name?" he asked.

The man hesitated, but finally he said, "Cole."

Reggie pulled on the man's coat, tugging him closer. "Kiss me again, Cole."

With a soft sigh, Cole did.

This time Reggie was a more active participant in the kiss. He stroked Cole's tongue with his own, followed when it retreated into Cole's mouth. Reggie made small sounds of want and need that Cole echoed. He raised his hands to grip Cole's shoulders. Slip into soft, sandy hair. Hold their faces close together.

He'd missed this so much. He'd convinced himself he didn't need another's touch, and now he realized how foolish he'd been.

It didn't matter that it was dangerous to be close to another man like this, or that he reminded Cole of a lover he had lost. Reggie needed this as much as he needed air and food and the creativity of acting.

"I want..." he said when their mouths parted. He shook his head, trying to form words into a coherent thought. "Please. Don't stop with this. It's been so long."

Cole rested his head against Reggie's

shoulder. He was breathing hard, too, and his hands hadn't left Reggie's body.

"Come with me," Cole said at last. "I've got a place not far from here." He kissed Reggie's neck. "For tonight. It's all I can offer."

Reggie didn't even hesitate. He'd think about tomorrow later.

CHAPTER NINE

Cole's place turned out to be little more than one of a number of rough, timber shacks within throwing distance of the Orphir mine.

This close to the mine, the air carried the stench of damp steam rising from the tunnels and the heavy, metallic smell of processed ore from the smokestacks. The smell permeated the small cabin, mixed with the smell of wood smoke from the stone fireplace and the aroma of the coffee and bacon Cole must have had for his last meal.

Cole lit an oil lamp that hung on a nail next

to the door. Warm, golden light illuminated the room, softening the edges of his stark living quarters.

The inside of the shack was as neat as anyone could make a room with a hard-packed dirt floor. The place was small, with barely enough room for the table and chairs in one corner, a chest of drawers that must have held Cole's clothes, a cabinet with a few mismatched dishes on top, and a narrow bed.

A pile of brushwood was stacked next to a stone fireplace. Cole had held Reggie's hand all the way to his place. He let go now only long enough to coax the smoldering embers in the fireplace into life. Reggie felt the heat begin to warm the chilly house.

As Cole worked the fire, Reggie tried to look anywhere but the bed. Several books lay on the table. Reggie started to pick one up when his attention was drawn to a leather portfolio. He lifted one edge of the scuffed leather.

"Please," Cole said, and Reggie understood he meant *don't*.

Reggie pulled his hand away from the portfolio. "I didn't mean..."

Cole stood up. "I'll show you anything you want, but I would ask that you let me explain why I..."

"You don't need to explain," Reggie said.

"I want you to know why I do..." Cole looked away from him then, stared at the flames. "The things I do, they have purpose. Meaning."

What was he talking about?

"Cole..."

Reggie crossed the short distance to stand next to Cole. He didn't need explanations, not now. What he needed was to feel Cole holding him again. Explanations could come later.

"I've been alone for a very long time," Reggie said. He touched Cole's arm, slid his hand around Cole's tense shoulder to the back of his neck. "I'm tired of being alone. I want to feel what I did when you kissed me, even if it's only for this one night."

Cole shivered under his touch. "I've been alone, too. I don't want you to think this is... that it's not you I think of when I kiss you. When I touch you."

He turned away from the fire to look at

Reggie. His eyes were the saddest Reggie had ever seen.

"You loved him very much, didn't you?"

"Yes."

A lot of pain lived in that one soft word. Reggie stroked the back of Cole's neck. "Was he an actor? Someone like me?"

Cole's ghost of a grin was sad and small. "No. He was a miner. Like I was."

Was. "You're not anymore?"

Cole hesitated. He glanced down, shook his head the slightest bit. "No."

Reggie stilled his hand on Cole's neck. He had never lost anyone like Cole had. He'd told Cole he didn't need explanations. He needed Cole to believe that.

"It hurts too much, I can see that," Reggie said. "I don't need to know." He pressed a kiss against Cole's shoulder. "You told me that it's me you see when you kiss and touch me, and I believe you. You don't have to tell me anything else."

"What I want to tell you..."

Cole lifted his head, took Reggie's head in his hands, and leaned in until their foreheads touched. Their breath mingled, their eyes so close nothing could be shielded from each other's gaze. It was the most incredibly intimate thing Reggie had ever experienced.

"No one has touched me since he died," Cole said. "I wanted no one. I talked to no one. And told no one the reason why. Until you." His thumb brushed the skin at Reggie's temple. "I may have first noticed you because you bear a resemblance. It's unavoidable. But you are the one I watched. You are the person I drew, not a ghost. You are the person here with me. No one else."

Reggie swallowed hard. This meant so much to Cole. He meant so much to Cole, and he didn't know if he deserved this. "Why? I've done nothing—"

Cole's kiss was quick. Chaste. "You awoke a heart I thought had died with him."

This was so much more than Reggie expected. The drawings had made him curious, made him want things he hadn't in a long time, but for Cole...

Reggie closed his eyes, the weight of the costume he still wore suddenly heavy on his shoulders. He wasn't in a play now; he couldn't walk off stage and get on with his life, not when he left this room. And when he did leave Virginia City after the company's run at Piper's Opera House was over—what then? Reggie hadn't thought beyond this moment. It had all happened so fast.

"I won't be staying," he murmured. "If we do this, it won't change that I'm an actor with a job, and I have to go where the job takes me."

"I understand," Cole said. "That's why I said only for tonight."

But did he really?

Cole backed away then.

Reggie took a deep, shaky breath while he watched Cole cross the room to stand by his bed.

The look Cole gave him smoldered hotter than the fire Cole had just rekindled. He didn't hold his hand out toward Reggie or open his arms wide, but the invitation couldn't be any clearer.

"When I first saw you, I didn't realize..." Cole turned his back to Reggie as he began to take off his clothes. "It wasn't until I saw you on stage that I noticed how similar you are to him."

"And that's when you began to draw me."

Reggie's legs felt numb as he went to stand behind Cole. He touched Cole's back, bare now, and was gratified to know he wasn't the only one trembling.

"Yes." Cole turned his head to look over his shoulder at Reggie. "Drawing you is how I discovered you touched my heart in your own right. It was the beginning of what I feel for you, Reggie. Only for you."

Reggie turned Cole around and kissed him, deep and needy and with a passion he hadn't felt for anyone else. Ever.

CHAPTER TEN

At first Reggie had simply felt curiosity about his mystery artist, then a sense of connection, and then longing to meet the man who'd drawn him in such fine, loving detail. Now he felt the pull of something deeper, and he needed—needed—to be with Cole.

Reggie fumbled with Cole's trousers and felt Cole's hands on him, removing the pieces of his costume as efficiently as if he wore nothing but a loose shirt and breeches.

When they were both finally, blissfully naked, Cole lay down on his bed. Reggie took a moment to look at him. Cole was beautiful in the flickering glow from the fire. Yes, he was too thin, and his skin was marred by old scars here and there, but he was muscular, and his cock curved thick and hard against his belly. Reggie was so hard himself just from the act of undressing each other that he ached.

He lay down next to Cole. The feel of Cole's body, naked against his own, made him shiver.

"I want you," he murmured. He kissed Cole's shoulder, mouthed the skin over Cole's collarbone as he trailed wet kisses toward Cole's neck. "So very much. From the first time I saw you at the party."

Cole's arms came around him then, and strong hands held him. "I was afraid to meet you in such a formal setting," he murmured in Reggie's ear. "The formalities required would have been beyond me."

"I looked for you."

"I know you did." One of Cole's hands drifted lower and cupped the curve of Reggie's backside, and Reggie moaned. "I watched you from where you could not see me."

Reggie was about to ask where that was when Cole shifted on the bed and Reggie found himself on top, resting on Cole's hard body, their cocks rubbing up against each other as Cole thrust up.

A deep, throbbing burn settled in Reggie's groin. He started rocking himself against Cole. Little noises in the back of his throat forced their way out of his mouth, mirrored in the sounds Cole was making. The hair on Cole's chest rubbed up against Reggie's smooth skin, grazing his nipples and teasing them even harder.

Reggie blindly sought out Cole's mouth. This time their kiss was wild, a clashing of lips and tongues and raw need. Their legs tangled together and their hands caressed and clutched at bare skin.

The air in the cabin was still chilly, but Reggie's skin burned, sweat trickling down the sides of his face, pooling along his spine. His hair came free from the leather thong he wore. He pulled the thong off and dropped it on the floor.

Cole spread his legs, and Reggie settled in

between. It felt so natural, so right. Like he belonged in this very spot and just didn't know it until now.

He wasn't going to last long, no matter how badly he wanted to take his time so that he could remember every single detail of their time together.

"Tell me what you want," Reggie murmured in Cole's ear, hoping that if he concentrated on Cole's needs, he could slow his own responses. "Let me know how to please you."

Cole moaned. "Touch me," he said. "Put your hands on me. I haven't felt another's touch in so long."

That Reggie could certainly do.

He had first touched another man when he'd been little more than a boy in London. The man had seemed huge to Reggie, hot and heavy in his hand. Cole was hot and heavy now. When Reggie touched Cole, the curl of his fist around that hard flesh wrung moans from them both.

But Reggie wanted more than just to touch. He kissed his way down Cole's body, lavished both nipples with attention from his tongue and gentle nips from his teeth, then continued his trail downward until his face was level with Cole's straining cock.

Cole smelled dark and musky and felt like velvet against Reggie's cheek. Reggie glanced up to find Cole watching him. Lamplight made his eyes glisten.

"You're beautiful," Reggie murmured, and then he put his mouth on Cole.

Cole's shout seemed to echo off the bare walls of the shack. Reggie whimpered himself. He'd forgotten how good the taste of another man was, but he was convinced that none before had ever tasted quite so right.

He worked his tongue and throat as he bobbed his head up and down Cole's hard flesh. Cole's hands came down to hold Reggie's head in place. Reggie grabbed his own aching cock and stroked himself as Cole thrust into his mouth.

"Reggie," Cole choked out.

Reggie understood it for the warning it was. He felt Cole's hands loosen on his head, but Reggie didn't move his mouth. If anything, he sucked harder.

The smell and taste of Cole's cock, the

AARON MICHAELS

sounds they both made—moans and grunts and whimpers—just the knowledge that he was giving Cole so much pleasure was enough for Reggie to find his own release. His cock pulsed in his hand even as Cole stiffened beneath him, clutching at Reggie's shoulders, and Reggie tasted a salty, bitter tang deep in his throat.

Once Cole was finished, he relaxed back on the bed as if all his muscles had gone liquid.

Reggie felt much the same. He wanted to curl up right where he was, but more than that, he wanted to kiss Cole again. To let the man know without words how deeply he felt about what had just happened between them.

Cole's eyes were half-opened, a lazy, satiated expression on his face marred only by the beginnings of a frown line between his brows.

"Reggie, I have something I—"

"Ssshh."

Reggie put his finger on Cole's lips to silence him.

Whatever Cole wanted to say, it could wait. He knew he'd told Cole they could talk later, but Reggie wanted his kiss and then he wanted just to feel, not talk. Not ruin the moment with

84

words that could be so easily misinterpreted.

When Reggie lowered his mouth to Cole's and cupped his face, Cole opened for him and kissed him back. Cole's hands stroked Reggie's arms up to his shoulders, held his head gently, then slid down his back. Cole's touch felt almost reverent. Reggie had never felt more cherished.

The kiss at last ended. Reggie stretched out beside Cole, his head pillowed on Cole's shoulder. Cole turned his head to look at Reggie, then reached down beside the bed and pulled up a rough blanket to cover them both. He wrapped his arm around Reggie and closed his eyes.

Reggie sighed, deeply content.

Cole's meaning was clear, even without words. Stay.

Reggie had no intention of leaving. He closed his own eyes and drifted off to sleep.

CHAPTER ELEVEN

Reggie woke to the sound of someone moving on the other side of Cole's door.

The fire had burned down to low embers. Cole must have doused the lamp after Reggie fell asleep, for the room was nearly charcoal dark.

Cole still lay with his arm wrapped around Reggie's shoulders. It was too dark to see Cole's expression, but his body was as tense as Reggie's own. Cole had heard the noise, too.

"Stay here," Cole whispered, and he kissed the side of Reggie's face. "When I get out of bed, cover yourself with the blanket."

Reggie nodded, and then he thought about the clothes they had left strewn on the floor. "Wait. My costume. If anyone sees it—"

"Sshh. I'll take care of it."

Now something scratched at the door. The walls of the house were thin, and the sound carried on the night air.

Cole's house was far enough away from the saloons and gambling halls that the night was almost deathly still. Reggie heard the muted sound of a distant owl and the soft whicker of a horse, and then a new sound came from the door. A rattle, short and furtive. It was almost like someone was testing the door latch.

Cole sat up, a dark silhouette against the banked fire. Reggie could tell he was pulling on his trousers and boots, then he shoved Reggie's clothes beneath the bed. Cole turned and pulled the blanket over Reggie's head, and the bed creaked as he got up.

Reggie tried to stay as quiet and still as possible. His breathing, confined as it was in the small space beneath the blanket, sounded too loud.

The rough wool blanket began to smell damp and earthy from the moisture in his breath. Reggie began to feel as if he couldn't breathe. Moving as little as possible, he rearranged the blankets to open up a small tunnel so he could breathe fresh air. The tunnel allowed him to see a small portion of the room beyond the blanket.

He was frightened—he could admit that. It would not be wise for him to be caught with Cole like this. While he didn't think the company would fire him, it might be the end of his appearances on stage, at least in Virginia City.

The consequences for Cole might be more dire. Although Cole had said he was no longer a miner, whatever he did in this city to provide for himself would no doubt be compromised if it became common knowledge that he slept with men.

So it should have come as no shock to Reggie when he saw Cole retrieve a gun from a saddlebag leaning against the wall next to the bed.

Except...

A shiver ran down Reggie's spine as he remembered the last time he'd seen a gun this close. In the low light from the fireplace, Reggie could only see the vaguest glint of the barrel, but he still had an eerie sense of deja vu.

Reggie heard as much as saw Cole slip toward the door. Even though Cole made little noise, dirt still crunched beneath his boots.

The person on the other side of the door must have heard it, too. A man's voice spoke a few short words, low and slurred and in a language Reggie didn't understand.

Cole responded in the same strange language. It wasn't the language the Chinamen spoke in San Francisco. While Reggie couldn't speak it, he'd learned to recognize the rhythm and sound of it. No, this was different, but somehow still familiar. The feeling of deja vu returned, even stronger this time.

Cole and the man on the other side of the door exchanged a few more words. Reggie could still see a glint of metal where Cole held the gun next to the door.

Cole stayed where he was when the conversation was over. Reggie held his breath and strained to hear anything outside of the blanket.

He thought he heard the sound of quiet foot-steps retreating away from the door, but it could have just been his imagination.

Eventually Cole came back to bed. He unfolded the blanket away from Reggie's face. "I'm sorry that happened," he said, his voice still low and with a tinge of the strange accent he'd had when he'd spoken to the man on the other side of the door.

"Are you all right?" Reggie asked. "Have I caused you trouble by being here?"

Cole shook his head as he sat on the edge of the bed. "No. I thought it best to be prepared, but this time it was only an old friend who wished to share his misery with me."

Reggie blinked. "I don't understand."

Cole looked down at the gun still in his hands. He slipped it back inside the saddlebag.

"He lost friends in the mine. Drink made him maudlin. He thought I would be someone to share his mood, but tonight, for once, I don't want to think about the mines."

Reggie didn't know what to say.

Instead of talking, he reached up to Cole's face. Cole turned his head to kiss the palm of

Reggie's hand.

"I think, perhaps, you should return to your hotel," Cole said. "As much as I want you to stay..." Cole touched Reggie's face, buried his fingers in Reggie's hair. "It would not be safe for you to be seen leaving here in the morning."

A huge part of Reggie wanted to stay, no matter the danger.

He felt comfortable with Cole. Cared for. If he couldn't stay, he wanted to come back.

No matter what they'd both said about this being only for this one night, he wanted to come back.

"I want to see you tomorrow," Reggie said. "After the performance."

Cole's fingers stilled in his hair. "I won't be here tomorrow."

What? "Where are you going?"

Cole abruptly got up from the bed. "I have a job to do. Gonna take some time to do it." He picked up a few pieces of kindling. "I would rather stay with you, but I have obligations."

He added the kindling to the fireplace and stirred the embers.

Reggie felt hot disappointment sting his

eyes. "Will I... can we see each other when you return?"

A small flame flared up in the fireplace. "I would like that," Cole said. "I'll let you know when I return."

"How?"

Cole turned his head to look at Reggie over his shoulder, and he smiled. "A small gift."

"Like the other things you've left me?"

"Perhaps. Or perhaps I'll bring you something more valuable."

More valuable. Cole didn't look like he was a man who had much money. "You don't have—"

"I want to."

The small ache in his chest unwound a little. Reggie was going to miss Cole while he was gone. He imagined the hours waiting for Cole to return might be the longest of his life. But Cole would come back, and he wanted to see Reggie again when he did. Whatever they had started here, it was going to last longer than this one night.

Reggie sat up in bed and smiled back. "If you're not going to be here tomorrow, I suppose we could..." He held up one side of the blanket. "It would be a shame to waste the opportunity."

Cole tilted his head to the side, and his smile widened. "Yes," he said. "It would."

CHAPTER TWELVE

Reggie stretched out on his bed, curled his toes beneath the fine, linen sheets. Morning sun made his room glow with soft, golden light, illuminating the new drawing from Cole that Reggie had propped up on the table beside his bed.

Before Reggie left Cole's home, Cole had opened the leather case and shown Reggie the drawings inside. Reggie had nearly been overwhelmed as he looked through sheet after sheet of Cole's artwork. Cole was an amazing artist. A few of the drawings were of various places

Reggie had seen in Virginia City: the Fourth Ward schoolhouse; the tall spires of St. Mary in the Mountains church; the granite headstones in the cemetery at the north edge of the city. Beautiful drawings that captured the feel of each of those places. But what took Reggie's breath away were the sheer number of drawings of him.

"Am I your muse?" he'd asked Cole, only half-teasing.

"You do inspire me," Cole had said. He kissed Reggie, slow and deep, and then told Reggie he could take a drawing with him if he wished.

Reggie thought he might have surprised Cole with the drawing he'd selected. It wasn't one of the myriad of drawings of himself, but rather a drawing of Virginia City as seen from near the summit of Mount Davidson. It reminded Reggie of the first glimpse he'd gotten of the city from the window of the stagecoach as it crested the summit.

He thought the city would always be special to him because this was where he made his stage debut. But he was wrong. What would always make this city special was Cole.

Cole walked Reggie nearly all the way back to his hotel. They stayed in the shadows, holding hands for most of the way. Cole had kissed him again, and then he was gone, blending into the dark night.

Reggie bunched the pillow beneath his head. He was pleasantly sore and incredibly aroused just thinking about what he and Cole had done only a few hours ago. He hadn't come to the city looking for a relationship, but he thought maybe he'd found one. Where it would go from here, he wasn't sure. One thing he was sure of—he was rapidly falling in love with Cole.

He traced a finger over the lines of the houses in the drawing. The paper was rough quality, like all the other drawings. It looked like unused newsprint. Did Cole work for the newspaper? Was that what was taking him out of town, a story he had to write?

At one time Mark Twain had written for the Territorial Enterprise, but he was long gone now. Reggie had only glanced through a few issues of the newspaper since he'd been here.

He didn't remember reading Cole's name, but then again he hadn't been looking.

Curiosity drove Reggie out of bed. He dressed quickly and went downstairs, this time more interested in finding a newspaper than eating breakfast. He found a copy of the current edition in the hotel lobby. He took it to his usual table and began to read.

The front page was still dominated by news of the cave-in at the Orphir mine. The articles called it a tragedy and reported on the arduous conditions in the mines. Another article mentioned that one of the local churches was seeking donations for the families of the men who died.

Reggie thought back to the conversation he'd heard the day before. None of the articles quoted the owner of the mine or any of the foremen, nor reported that the owner had made any provision for the families of the men who died.

Inside the newspaper, the articles were primarily devoted to social events, including a large article about the Shakespeare company's performances at the opera house.

Reggie scanned through the articles looking for Cole's name, but he didn't see it anywhere.

"So much for that idea," he murmured.

It was somewhat disconcerting to have made love to such a mysterious man. And not only made love, but to find himself falling in love with someone he knew so little about. What did Cole do for a living? Or had he made enough money as a miner that he only needed to work sporadically? He didn't live like a rich man, at least not any rich man Reggie had ever seen.

Reggie was still reading the newspaper—an editorial calling for the sheriff to make greater efforts to catch the stagecoach robber—when Vivian and Blanche came down to breakfast. Blanche sat down at a table, but Vivian came over to stand next to Reggie.

"You left in quite a hurry last night," she said.

She pulled on the finger of one glove, seemingly giving it her undivided attention. Reggie knew better. She was building up to something she wanted to tell him.

He kept his attention on the newspaper and

didn't say anything. Just because he'd saved her from being robbed didn't mean he enjoyed her games.

"In your costume," she said. When he still said nothing, she stopped playing with her glove and sighed, rather dramatically, Reggie thought. "I'm trying to be nice to you."

"And I appreciate it." Reggie looked up from his paper. "Although I'm not sure why you feel the need to be nice."

"Because if I noticed you chased after someone leaving the box after you played to the very same box all night, I'm sure other people noticed as well," she said, her voice low. "And unless you were running off after someone like me, I don't think you want anyone noticing the person you were really chasing after." Her voice dropped even lower. "Or that when you came back to your room, your costume was... shall I say—rather disheveled?"

She knew.

Reggie went cold. "I don't think it's any of your business."

Her expression changed from haughty and annoyed to something almost like sympathy. "I have been where you are, whether or not you believe me. I didn't start out intending to have this life, but when you fall for someone... 'inappropriate'... your life can change in—"

Her eyes filled with unshed tears, the first time Reggie had ever seen her nearly in tears when it wasn't called for on stage. She shook her head and tried to smile. "You've been nice to me when you had no reason. I believe this settles my debt for your kindness to me."

And with that she walked away, not even stopping to sit with Blanche.

CHAPTER THIRTEEN

Trying to find Cole was not the smartest thing Reggie had ever done. In fact, it ranked right up there with leaving home at fourteen in the company of a man who promised to tutor him in acting and who ended up only wanting Reggie to use his looks to steal to earn his keep.

He had to find Cole. Reggie had to tell Cole not to come to the theater again. Not to leave anything as a signal that he was back.

If Vivian had told the truth—and Reggie had no reason to believe she hadn't, not this time—she wasn't the only one who knew Reggie had chased after Cole last night. Was she the only one who had seen him come back to the hotel, still in his costume? Had anyone seen the two of them walking in the shadows? Holding hands?

The warm glow Reggie had woken with had been replaced by a nervous dread. For whatever reason, Cole was a secretive man. Reggie didn't want Cole hurt by what they'd done.

Reggie wished he'd paid more attention last night when Cole had led him back to the hotel. The streets looked different in the daylight. Reggie tried to recreate his steps, but he felt like he was becoming increasingly lost.

How he could ever hope to find Cole's house again? All the houses in this section of town looked like the shack Cole lived in.

Frustrated, he kept walking, resisting the urge to run. He didn't want to draw attention to himself. At least not any more than he already had. Most of the men he passed on the street appeared to be miners—thin, their skin pale beneath layered dirt and haggard beards, their clothes threadbare and filthy. Reggie stood out in his clean clothes, neatly trimmed goatee, his hair pulled back at the base of his neck. He hunched his shoulders and shoved his hands in his coat pocket and kept walking.

He found Cole rather abruptly and unexpectedly. Reggie crossed a narrow street and rounded the back corner of a stable, intending to cross behind the paddocks to another narrow street, when he saw Cole near the rear doors of the stable holding the reins of a sturdy bay mare.

Cole was dressed in a scuffed leather jacket and dark trousers, with well-worn chaps on his legs and a six-gun belted around his waist. He was talking to another man—a wiry man with a leather apron covering his belly and his arms glistening with sweat. The stable owner perhaps, or a smithy?

Reggie wasn't close enough to hear what Cole and the blacksmith were talking about, but Cole didn't appear to be happy. The corners of his mouth were turned down, and when the smithy leaned forward to say something close to Cole's ear, Cole shook his head, a quick, angry gesture.

Reggie waited until Cole and the blacksmith were done talking and the other man had gone back inside the stables. Cole started to saddle the bay mare. Reggie took a deep breath and walked over to where Cole stood.

Cole must have heard Reggie's boot steps on the rocky dirt. He glanced up, surprise widening his eyes.

"Reggie?"

Reggie smiled, nervous now as Cole glanced toward the back door of the stable where the smithy had disappeared, and then around himself as if to see who might be watching.

"You shouldn't be here," Cole said, turning his attention back to cinching the saddle on his horse. "I'm happy to see you, but this is not wise."

Reggie kept his distance even though he wanted to walk right up to Cole, wanted the same hugs and kisses they'd shared the night before.

"I needed to tell you..." Reggie cleared his throat. "One of the actresses saw me last night. She warned me this morning, and I—"

"Will she say anything?" Cole asked.

Reggie felt pinned by the intensity of Cole's stare. Here, in the daylight, Cole's eyes were an icy blue, and Reggie could imagine how chilling it must be to look in those eyes when Cole was truly angry.

"No," Reggie said. "At least I don't think so. I did a favor for her recently. She told me this settled our debt. I just wanted to warn you not to come back to the opera house, not to leave me things." Reggie remembered the boy who had delivered the first drawing. "At least not personally," he said, and he smiled a nervous smile, still somewhat unsettled by the hard edge to Cole's gaze. "I would miss them though."

"As I would miss giving them to you." Cole looked away, as if he was uncomfortable looking at Reggie when he made such an admission.

"The boy... he..." Reggie didn't know how to ask if the boy could be trusted. He didn't want to insult anyone, much less a boy, but Cole had asked about Vivian.

"He is the son of a friend, someone who has known me for a long time. We can trust him."

We.

Reggie didn't think he'd ever felt so good hearing such a simple word. "I wish..." He sighed. He knew what he wished for. Time—and a comfortable, quiet, secluded bed where he could stretch out next to Cole and make love for days on end. Such was not reality. "I wish you good journey," Reggie said instead.

Cole fastened the straps of the saddlebags Reggie had seen the night before, cinching everything tight. He paused when the blacksmith appeared at the stable door carrying a rifle.

"Stay," Cole murmured to Reggie. "It would look worse if you left suddenly."

Reggie nodded, tense again. He tried to paste a neutral expression on his face.

"Hey, you're one of them actors at the opera house, ain't ya?" the blacksmith said as he walked over to where Cole stood and handed him the rifle.

"Yes," Reggie said. He didn't volunteer anything else. He wanted to let Cole make whatever explanations were appropriate.

"Long way away from that end of town." The smithy stood with his hands on his hips, his bare head tilted to one side, examining Reggie as if he was looking at horseflesh.

"I walk about the city every day," Reggie said. "I like to explore when I'm in new places."

"We met at the reception opening night," Cole said. "He spotted me and wanted to say hello."

The smithy watched the two of them, eyes moving back and forth. "Guess it's hard to make friends when you travel a lot," he said.

"It isn't easy," Reggie said.

"Huh." The man nodded at Cole's horse. "About time you get a move on, don't you think?" he asked Cole.

"It'll just be another minute," Cole said.

"Huh," the smithy said again. With one more glance at Reggie, he turned around and walked back inside the dark stable.

What had just happened, and why did Reggie have a feeling the blacksmith was more than just someone who stabled Cole's horse? Why had the blacksmith given Cole a rifle when Cole had his own gun?

"What was that about?" Reggie asked.

Cole slid the barrel of the rifle into a leather holster attached to the saddle. "Nothing you need to worry about," Cole said, but he wouldn't meet Reggie's eyes with his own. "I have to go."

Reggie stepped back as Cole mounted the horse.

Cole's coat fanned out behind him, and there, stuffed half into the back pocket of Cole's trousers, was something that made Reggie's blood turn to ice.

CHAPTER FOURTEEN

It wasn't much. Just a bit of burlap cloth. But it was enough that Reggie knew, and everything suddenly fell into place.

"It was you," Reggie said.

His lips felt numb, his voice ancient, but he couldn't stop himself.

"You robbed me." He looked up at Cole's face with wide, shocked eyes. "You held a gun on me and took my money. You took my father's—" Watch. And then had given it back. Why? Because he felt guilty?

Because Cole had grown to care about

Reggie and felt bad for what he'd done?

Cole looked like he was going to be sick. "Reggie, no. I—"

Reggie shook his head. "No! You left me penniless in a strange city. I thought you might kill me, kill us all."

He couldn't reconcile the gentle man he'd made love with the night before with the bandit who'd been ruthless enough to hold up a stage single-handedly. But the clues were all there. The ease with which Cole had handled the gun the night before. The accent he'd used when speaking with the man at his front door. And the damning burlap mask shoved in his pocket.

The stage was leaving again, and Cole was leaving town to do a job. He was going to rob the coach.

What would he do to Reggie now that Reggie had figured out who he was?

Reggie wasn't about to wait to find out. He turned and ran.

He fled down the street and through narrow yards to get away from Cole just like he'd run down alleys and passageways the night before chasing after Cole. Reggie's heart hammered in his chest as he heard the pounding of hooves behind him. He tried to run faster, but it was inevitable that Cole would catch him.

Reggie supposed he should be grateful that Cole didn't just shoot him. Instead, Cole leapt from the horse and fell on Reggie's shoulders, knocking them both to the ground.

Reggie couldn't breathe. Cole was a heavy weight against his back, the rocky ground solid beneath him. Reggie lay on his stomach, trying to suck air into his lungs and not panic when he couldn't.

Cole rolled off of him and maneuvered both of them into the shade of a nearby house. Scrub brush at the side of the house hid them from easy view.

"Relax," Cole said. He held Reggie spooned against his chest, his face nestled into Reggie's hair. "I won't hurt you, I swear. I just want a chance to explain, then I'll let you go to do what you will. But you have to relax so you can breathe."

Gentle fingers smoothed Reggie's hair away from his face. Reggie tried to let go of his fear, but his entire body felt jarred and sore, and he thought he could feel the butt of Cole's gun digging into his hip.

Gradually Reggie's chest loosened, and he gulped in deep, burning breaths of air. The dusty smell of sagebrush made him want to sneeze.

"Easy," Cole said. "You're all right."

Cole said some words then in the language he'd spoken last night. It could have been an endearment, but Reggie couldn't be sure. Cole's fingers were still gentle on his face.

Reggie wanted so much for the last few minutes to never have happened, but he couldn't undo it now. The most Reggie could do was listen and hope that Cole would be true to his word.

"What... what language is that?" Reggie asked. He had to clear his throat in order to get the question out, and his chest hurt, but at least he was breathing and talking again.

"Basque," Cole said. "Some of the men in the mines come from shepherding families to the north. It's their language."

"It's what you spoke last night."

"Yes."

Cole was still stroking his head. "What did you just say to me?" Reggie asked.

Reggie felt Cole place a soft kiss on the back of his head. He thought his heart might break. How could this have gone so wrong?

"I can't translate it," Cole said. "It's a name someone would call a lover—a person held close to the heart."

Reggie closed his eyes against the hot burn of tears. "Is that what I am to you?"

Another kiss. "Yes," Cole murmured, his head resting against the back of Reggie's.

Reggie reached up to touch Cole's hand where Cole held him tight. "Is it just for the money? Is that why... Am I such a horrible judge of character that I've fallen in love with a man who kills people for money?"

Cole's head dropped against Reggie's shoulder. Reggie heard the impatient sound of Cole's horse shaking its head, snorting and pawing at the dry dirt. He heard children's laughter and barking dogs and the chattering of birds in scattered bushes between houses.

"I never killed anyone," Cole said softly. "I only rob those who can afford to lose their money and possessions, to make sure that those who have nothing can survive a while longer."

Reggie wasn't wealthy. None of the actors were. How dare Cole make that kind of judgment!

"I couldn't afford—" Reggie stopped himself when the rest of what Cole said sank in. He turned around to look Cole in the face. "What do you mean, for those who have nothing?"

Reggie was shocked when Cole raised his head. Cole's eyes were red-rimmed, and even though he hadn't cried, he looked about as close as a man could get to crying without spilling tears.

"The men who die in the mine," Cole said. "They leave families behind. I gave them what I could, and when I had nothing left, I began to take it from the man who had taken everything from them." He touched Reggie's face. "I took from you before I knew what you would come to mean to me. I wanted to tell you last night, but I... If I could undo what I did to you on that coach, I would. Don't be afraid of me. Please."

Understanding swept through Reggie. Cole wouldn't hurt him. Cole was the Western embodiment of an old English folk tale.

"Robin Hood," Reggie murmured.

Cole blinked. "Who is..."

"An old story about a man who robs from the rich to give to the poor, although some would call him a mere criminal." Reggie cupped the side of Cole's face. "It appears I've fallen in love with Robin Hood."

CHAPTER FIFTEEN

Cole blinked again. "In love?" His gaze held Reggie's, and he was breathing hard. "You've fallen in love with me?"

Reggie hadn't meant to make the admission, but he wasn't about to deny it either. "Yes."

He leaned forward and kissed Cole gently on the lips, not caring in that moment that they might be watched.

The kiss ended all too quickly.

Cole looked over Reggie's shoulder. Apparently satisfied that the bushes hid them sufficiently, he kissed Reggie again, deeper and more thoroughly, although just as quickly.

"I love you, too, Reggie. But I have to go."

What?

"How can you still do this?" Cole tried to get to his feet, but Reggie pushed him back against the building. "You can't rob more innocent people."

"I have to—"

"No! This is not right, no matter what your reason."

"Please move." Cole grabbed Reggie's hands and held them away from himself. "I need to—"

"No. I won't let you!"

"I don't have a choice!" Cole stopped fighting and slumped against the building. "It's no longer my decision. It hasn't been for a long time."

Reggie let go of him. "What do you mean?"

Cole looked back the way they had come. "I was discovered by someone who doesn't care about me as you do." Cole shut his eyes. "In exchange for my freedom, I have to pay him. If I don't, he'll identify me to the sheriff, and I'll be hanged."

Oh, god. Cole was being blackmailed.

"Reggie, I have to go."

Cole opened his eyes and gently touched the side of Reggie's face. "I promise I'll return to you, and then we can decide what to do, but for today I have to—"

"You can't." The conversation he'd had the night before with the stagecoach driver came back to Reggie, as clear as if it was dialogue he'd rehearsed for a new play. A tragic love story where the hero's lover dies in the last act. "You'll be killed. They're laying a trap for you."

Reggie explained what the stagecoach driver had told him. Cole initially looked shocked and then increasingly angry. He pushed Reggie off his lap, and this time Reggie let him. Cole stalked over to his horse and removed the rifle from its holster. He opened the chamber, peered inside, and swore.

"It would have exploded if I shot it," Cole said. "It might not have killed me, but it would have kept me from fighting back if I was ambushed."

The blacksmith had given Cole the rifle. Was he in on the trap? But if he was, that meant that he—

"The smithy's the one who's been black-mailing you," Reggie said.

Cole nodded. "Cummings put a price on my head. It must have finally gotten high enough." He threw the rifle on the ground. "Even though he took his pound of flesh from me, he left me with enough to give to those who truly need it. I thought he understood."

"You can't go, not now."

Cole's eyes looked hollow. "If I don't, families will starve. I promised..." Cole shook his head.

Reggie wanted so much to hold Cole and comfort him, but as soon as Cole stood up, the illusion of privacy was gone. He felt like every empty window hid someone watching them, so he stroked Cole's horse instead.

"Why did you promise?" Reggie asked. He already knew what Cole had promised; now what Reggie needed to know was why.

"I survived."

Cole sighed. It was such a forlorn sound,

Reggie wanted to cry. He made himself stare at the way the individual hairs on the horse's shoulder slid beneath the palm of his hand as he stroked her.

"Nine of us worked the deepest shafts in the Orphir," Cole said. "Setting timbers, chasing a vein that was already near mined out. Grover and I, we'd been together for about a year by then, keeping what we were to each other to ourselves. His family was pretty important around here at the time, and we didn't want..."

Cole cleared his throat, rubbed the back of his neck. When he started speaking again, his voice had a far-off quality, like how a man might talk about a nightmare that scared him senseless in the middle of the night but seemed somehow less real in the light of day.

"That day it was Grover and me and the other seven, just like any other day. The ground down there's not as solid as you might think. So much ore's been taken out over the years, what's left shifts and moves, crumbles right around you. Dirt sifts through the cracks between timbers. Wood groans with the weight of it. Steam fills the tunnels from cracks in the ground beneath you. The sound of shovels and picks is constant. When the tunnel collapsed on us, the timbers gave way without any warning. The lanterns went out. Dust and steam was thick enough to choke on. Damn place felt like the inside of a grave." Cole shook his head. "I got out. They didn't."

Reggie did cry then, imagining it. Cole had lost his lover and his closest mates in an accident that could have taken his life, too. Reggie gripped a handful of the mare's mane and squeezed tight to keep himself quiet.

"Men still die in the mines," Cole said. "No provision is made for their families, even though that bastard Cummings sits in his fancy house with more wealth than he needs for five lifetimes." He scuffed the toe of his boot in the dirt. "So I took what he refused to give and made sure it got to the people that needed it, and for that they'll hang me if I'm caught."

Reggie knew all too well what would happen to Cole if he was caught. A powerful man like Cummings would see Cole hang no matter what Cole's motivations.

"You can't go today," Reggie said. "You

must see that."

Cole nodded. "That I do. But if I don't go, the result's the same. I'll get turned in, and it won't matter in the end whether they can prove I did it or not."

"It doesn't have to be that way." Reggie sniffled, tried to get himself under control. "There has to be something else we can do."

He knew they couldn't take down Cummings. Reggie had no illusions about that. But the smithy was the immediate threat. There had to be a way to stop him from telling what he knew.

All they needed was some time to think and to come up with a plan.

CHAPTER SIXTEEN

They spent the afternoon together in Cole's small house. Cole cooked a simple meal for the two of them—pan biscuits along with a chicken roasted on a spit in the fireplace. They fed each other and then made love until they couldn't move, and afterward Cole napped. Reggie curled around him and held him and tried to come up with a plan.

Cole had told him the most important thing, even beyond his freedom or his own life, was to keep his promise to the widows of the men who'd died in the mines.

Not all of the widows still lived in Virginia City. Some had moved on, packed up their children and what belongings they could carry and ridden the stage to find new lives with friends and family elsewhere. But there were always new widows, more fatherless children, and Cole had been providing for them all. First with the money he'd earned mining, and then with the money he'd stolen from Cummings' stages after Cole found he could no longer stand to earn his money below ground. He'd seen the stagecoach robberies as poetic justice.

"I am sorry about robbing you," Cole had told him. "I wish I could give you your money back, but it's gone. All I had left to return to you was your watch."

Reggie had forgiven him after first making Cole promise that his stagecoach robbing days were over. "And thank you for not taking Vivian's money."

"You were quite the hero." Cole had been reclining naked on his bed, his hand tracing lazy circles on Reggie's belly. "It did make me wonder if you... and she..."

He'd left the question unasked, but Reggie

had recognized it for what it was.

"No, that's something that never... not for lack of trying on her part, understand, but for lack of interest on mine." Reggie had taken Cole's hand and kissed each of his worn knuckles. "This is all that interests me."

"My hand?"

They had laughed and loved and not thought any further ahead than the next kiss. But now that Reggie was watching Cole sleep, the future was all he could think about.

The smithy was a greedy man. He hadn't turned Cole in, preferring instead to take a size-able amount of what should have gone to provide for the widows and their children. What had made the smithy change his mind? Did he think Cole was about to be caught and decided to help that happen?

If Reggie was going to get Cole out from under the threat the smithy posed, he would have to trap the man, and do it in such a way that he could trust the smithy to keep what he knew about Cole to himself. And for good measure, Reggie wanted to benefit the people Cole had been helping, for there would be no more help from their own personal Robin Hood.

The answer, when it came to Reggie, was so simple he wondered why he didn't think of it earlier. "You're thick, Grayson," he muttered to himself. Reggie pulled Cole closer and pressed a kiss to his shoulder. Cole murmured in his sleep and snuggled against Reggie, but didn't wake.

Reggie closed his eyes against the afternoon sun. He'd need his sleep. He'd need to be alert tonight if he had a chance in hell of convincing the rest of the San Francisco Shakespeare Company to go along with his plan.

"You want us to what?" Jeremiah said.

"Put on a benefit performance," Reggie said. "An open-air festival. We could invite the townspeople to participate if they wished."

"And we wouldn't be paid for this," Blanche said, leaning back in the chair in front of Reggie's dressing table.

Reggie had gathered his fellow actors as they were getting ready for the evening's performance. Blanche was half in and half out of costume, and Jeremiah had a nearly empty bottle of whiskey with him—leftover from the night before, if his current level of alertness was any indication. Vivian stood next to Jeremiah, her arms crossed in front of her.

"No," Reggie said. "The money would go to the families of the men who just died in the mines."

Jeremiah and Blanche stared at him as if he'd gone daft, but Vivian had a more calculating look on her face. "Why do you care, Reggie?" she asked. "In another week, we'll be leaving this city behind. You'll never see these people again."

It was only another week. Reggie had plans about that as well, but he wasn't going to tell anyone just yet. Not even Cole.

Cole had left before Reggie returned to the opera house. Reggie had convinced him to ride off into the hills so the smithy would think Cole had gone to rob the stagecoach as planned. Reggie hoped by the time the smithy heard the news that the stagecoach had made its way to Reno unscathed, Cole's problems with the smithy would be long over.

"It's the right thing to do." Reggie spoke to all of them, but he kept his gaze locked with Vivian's. "This city suffered a loss. The people who work here are no different than us. They've come to our performances and taken us in when some of us had no means to repay them. It's our turn to help."

Vivian's eyes narrowed, and for a moment Reggie was afraid she was going to tell the others what she knew about him. But then she nodded.

"Reggie's right," she said. "I know what it's like to go to sleep with an empty belly, unlike you." She nudged Jeremiah's boot with her toe and smiled at him to deflect her sarcasm. "This will be fun."

"Fun." Jeremiah grunted and lifted his bottle. "Buy me a bottle, Mr. Grayson, and I'll put on a show like you've never seen."

Reggie had no doubt of that. "So you'll help me convince our esteemed director to let the company do this?"

Jeremiah and Vivian nodded. Blanche stroked the vial that dangled at the end of her necklace. Reggie wondered if she'd found a new supplier for the "holy water" she kept inside.

"Well, I suppose if you all want to do this," Blanche said, "I don't want to seem like the only skinflint. Tell me what to do."

Reggie grinned. "I wanted us all to propose this together, after tonight's performance."

"Then I suppose we should give such a performance that the man will have no choice but to agree." Jeremiah took a healthy swig from his bottle. "Come, m'dear," he said to Blanche. "I would offer my services with respect to your costume."

Blanche chuckled, a deep, throaty sound. "Now, now, my dear Mr. Sommersby. When have I ever needed your assistance getting into costume?"

Jeremiah leaned in close to her ear. "I don't recall offering to help you into costume," he said in a stage whisper.

Blanche swatted him on the arm, but she put her hand in the crook of his elbow. Reggie watched the two of them leave his dressing room.

When Vivian started to follow, Reggie

touched her elbow.

"I have something more I need to ask of you," he said.

CHAPTER SEVENTEEN

It took two days to organize an outdoor festival, complete with an amateur talent show and a performance by the company of a previously unknown one-act play about the bandit hero, Robin Hood.

Previously unknown only because Reggie had to write it.

He'd taken what little he knew of the legend of Robin Hood and written a scene in which Robin's lover pleads with the sheriff to spare Robin's life. Jeremiah had the part of the sheriff, Vivian was the fair, young maiden who had fallen in love with the thief, and Reggie—in what he thought of as a private tribute to Cole and what his fellow actors thought was a tad bit too much ego—cast himself as Robin Hood.

Blanche was not happy to be a mere lady in waiting until Reggie told her she would play a pivotal part when she seduced the sheriff, thus allowing the lovers to escape.

Reggie introduced himself to the man who ran the newspaper, and along with no small amount of flirtatious behavior on Vivian's part, convinced the man to print a good number of playbills for the benefit performance, which was to be held in a vacant lot next to St. Mary in the Mountains Church. Attendance was free, but everyone was encouraged to bring either what money they could afford or what food they could donate, all of which would be divided equally among the miners' families at the end of the day.

Reggie and Vivian personally delivered a playbill to the smithy. Vivian flirted with the smithy, as Reggie requested. She looked at him from beneath her lashes, touched him on the arm, and told him she hoped to see him in the audience. The man had been sufficiently distracted that Reggie was able to not only paste the playbill on the front of the stables without the man even noticing, but take a few moments to do what he needed to do inside the stables as well.

"Thank you," he murmured to Vivian as they walked away, passing out playbills to those people on the street who would take them.

Vivian pulled on the finger of her glove. "I'm not sure I ever want you to save me again, although this should definitely settle our debt. He wasn't a very nice man."

"No," Reggie said. "He isn't."

"And I don't want to know why you had me do that."

"No, you don't."

"I'm taking a lot here on faith, Reggie."

He leaned over and kissed her on the cheek, a quick peck.

She blushed, and the corners of her mouth turned up. "If I didn't already know..." She shook her head a little and gave him a quick, amused glance. "I suppose all future kisses will be confined to the stage. More's the pity."

Not from Reggie's point of view. He wished he could tell her about Cole. About how wonderful he was, how kind-hearted. What a marvelous kisser—and lover—he was. But camaraderie only went so far.

So instead Reggie offered Vivian his arm and they went on their way, passing out playbills and chatting about the new parts Reggie had created. All the while, Reggie thought he could feel the smithy's eyes on them.

Good. It was just what Reggie wanted.

"He's here," Vivian whispered to Reggie.

Reggie felt his stomach flutter with more than the usual nerves he felt before he went on stage. The smithy was in the audience. With any luck, he would attempt to see Vivian after the performance, when Vivian had one more part to play. If this worked, Reggie—and Cole—would end up deeply in her debt.

"Are you sure you can do this?" Reggie asked.

Vivian arched an eyebrow. "I may look young and helpless," she said, "but as long as he doesn't hold a gun on me, I'll be fine."

The benefit so far had been a marvelous success. The talent show had drawn both the truly horrible as well as the surprisingly good. Reggie's favorite so far had been a young boy and his sister who performed artfully done magic tricks. He'd applauded as loudly as the rest of the audience when the boy bowed and his sister curtsied before running off stage to their obviously proud mother.

While Reggie might have thought of the idea for the benefit and made the initial arrangements, the townspeople had embraced the idea and expanded on it. One of the local saloons sponsored box lunches for the first hundred people who asked for them. Other businesses followed suit, donating food and drink both to the widows and their families as well as those in attendance, or raffling off goods and services. From the look of the no longer empty field, a good third of the population of Virginia City had turned out to see the play and the amateur performances.

Reggie wished Cole could have been there to see it. Even though he'd only spent two days—well, one night and almost all of the following day—with Cole, Reggie missed him greatly. His bed felt too large and lonely. He found himself wanting to talk to Cole, wanting to tell Cole about what he'd done and seen or about nothing at all, or just listen to Cole talk. He wanted to know all about Cole. Where he'd traveled, what he'd seen, the interesting people he'd met. Reggie hoped when this was over, he'd have enough time with Cole to do all that and more.

The company stood off to the side of the makeshift stage, which was just a patch of bare ground at the top of a small rise next to the side of the church. A few bench seats from the church had been moved outside for stage dressing. The audience sat on blankets and coats spread out on the dusty ground.

"Are you ready, young Robin Hood?" Blanche asked.

Reggie nodded. What with worrying about whether the smithy would actually attend the benefit, he hadn't had much time to even think about his performance.

The first performance of the very first play

he'd ever written.

He really wished Cole could be there to see it.

The parish priest came up to the actors and patted Reggie on the shoulder. "Break a leg, isn't that the saying?"

Reggie gave the priest a nervous grin. The priest had been the most enthusiastic among all the people Reggie had spoken to about the benefit, and not just because the benefit would help the neediest families in his parish. Reggie wondered if the priest would have liked to be in the play, and he'd considered writing a part for a friar.

Vivian had talked him out of it. "You have enough to worry about," she'd said.

"It is indeed," Reggie said. "Thank you, Father."

"Then let us take the stage, before I clap you in irons," Jeremiah said.

Jeremiah had really taken to his role as sheriff. He'd borrowed a badge from one of the city's deputies and found a long, black leather coat that made him look rather dangerous.

All of the costumes were makeshift. Reggie

had borrowed bits and pieces from various costumes he wore on stage, as had Blanche. Vivian had a new dress of rich, burgundy wool. Reggie wasn't sure he wanted to know how she'd managed to find a dress that actually looked like it belonged on a British maiden of yesteryear. As she said, she really wasn't young and helpless. Perhaps she had admirers of her own who weren't averse to showering her with signs of affection.

Reggie walked on the makeshift stage with Vivian to enthusiastic applause, along with cheers and gasps from the children. Reggie had never performed in front of so many children before. He hadn't really thought about whether children would be able to understand the play. He hoped the short performance wouldn't bore them.

As it turned out, the children seemed to enjoy the performance as much as their parents. They cheered for Robin Hood, booed the sheriff, and laughed at the antics of the lady in waiting trying to get the sheriff to notice her.

When the sheriff finally did fall under the lady in waiting's spell, Reggie thought that

Blanche and Jeremiah over-played their kiss just a bit, but at least it looked convincing. Reggie and Vivian exited the stage and disappeared within the church to cheers from the audience, and then the play was over.

Vivian's cheeks were flushed with excitement as they waited inside the church for Jeremiah and Blanche to join them before they all went out to take their final bows. "You might have a career as a playwright," she told him.

"I'd rather be an actor."

He rubbed the palms of his hands on the front of his costume. Although, if truth be told, it had been gratifying to think that the audience had responded so well to a play that hadn't even existed until he wrote it.

After Reggie took his bows with his fellow actors, he and Vivian went out in the audience to talk to the people who wanted to meet them and thank them for attending. Reggie had hoped that Jeremiah and Blanche would join them, but they disappeared after the applause ended, no doubt to finish the scene somewhere in private.

Reggie tried to keep track of Vivian. He soon realized it would be impossible unless he stayed right next to her, and that might discourage the smithy from approaching her. Reggie, in his Robin Hood costume, proved very popular with the children. They all wanted to touch him, or tell him something about their lives, or ask him what a thief had to eat for dinner. Reggie almost told them biscuits and chicken, but stopped himself. He was still feeling somewhat euphoric from the performance. He didn't want to forget that the business with the smithy was deadly serious.

A young boy of no more than eight pulled on the sleeve of Reggie's costume.

"Is the maiden your girlfriend?" the boy asked.

Reggie smiled at him. "She's Robin Hood's girlfriend, that's true," Reggie said. "But they must keep it a secret for the sheriff wants badly to arrest Robin."

"Then why is she leaving with that man?" asked another boy, taller and older than the first, but with a strong family resemblance.

Reggie looked to where the boys were pointing. He barely saw the top of Vivian's head. At her side was the smithy. The man seemed to be steering Vivian away from the crowd.

That wasn't part of the plan, not at all.

"I think the fair maiden needs to be res-cued," Reggie told the children, trying hard not to let them see how frightened for Vivian he was. "Will you excuse me?"

The boys nodded. Reggie made his way through the crowd as quickly as he could. He didn't want to lose sight of Vivian. If anything happened to her because of...

Don't think that way, he told himself.

He saw the smithy guide Vivian toward the street that ran sharply down an incline behind the church. By the time Reggie reached the street, the smithy, with Vivian in tow, was rounding the corner the next street over. They were running, the smithy pulling Vivian along by the hand. The few people on the street turned to watch them, but no one tried to stop them.

Reggie started running after them. He prayed he wouldn't be too late.

CHAPTER EIGHTEEN

Reggie should have known the smithy would go back to the stables.

He reached the stable door just as the smithy started to swing it shut. He held Vivian with a fist in her hair. Vivian was fighting him, but the smithy was strong from years spent in his trade, and her blows had no effect.

Reggie barreled into the door. Only his momentum made it swing inward.

The smithy stumbled backward, dragging Vivian along with him. Instead of letting her go, he wrapped an arm around her neck and held her close to him. Reggie felt himself go cold as he saw a wicked looking, sharply pointed tool in the smithy's other hand. The smithy held the tool against Vivian's throat.

"Just how dumb do you two think I am?" the smithy said.

Vivian's eyes were wide. "I don't know what you—"

"Shut up!" The smithy pressed the sharp point of the tool to Vivian's throat, and she winced. "Thought you were gonna frame me, huh? You think I was too stupid to know your name, make the connection?"

Grayson. His father's name was engraved inside the watch.

Reggie's heart sank. He had planted the watch in the stable to make it look like it had fallen from someone's pocket. Vivian was sup-posed to ask the smithy the time, and when the man showed off the watch he'd found in his stable, Vivian and then Reggie would denounce him as the stagecoach bandit.

In a way the smithy was the bandit, or at least Reggie had told his conscience that when he devised this plan. He'd never explained the specifics to Cole. He wasn't sure Cole would have agreed to let him implicate the smithy in the robberies.

"She had nothing to do with it," Reggie said. "Please let her go."

He wondered if the smithy had found the other thing he'd left in the stables—Cole's burlap mask. He wasn't sure if Cole knew that Reggie had taken the mask when he'd left Cole's house.

The smithy smiled. "And now why should I do that?"

The sound of a hammer being cocked was unmistakable. "Because I said so."

Cole!

Reggie's jaw dropped. How did Cole get there? And how did he know where to be?

The smithy's smile vanished. Cole was standing inside an empty stall near the front of the stables, his gun drawn. The heavy stall railing had been gnawed by countless horses over the years. The barrel of Cole's gun rested in shallow scallop in the wood, the cold steel pointed at the smithy's head.

"Let the lady go," Cole said. "Let them both

go. This matter's between you and me. Always has been, and it's time to put an end to it."

"With you holding a gun on me? I don't think so."

The smithy backed toward the rear of the stables, dragging Vivian along with him. The heels of her shoes scuffed the dirt, raising dust and the musty, dank smell of manure.

Cole followed the smithy with the barrel of his gun. Reggie started to follow as well.

"Stay where you are, Reggie." Cole's voice was low and serious.

Reggie stopped in his tracks when he saw why.

The inside of the stables was cramped and crowded with all manner of things as if the smithy had saved everything he'd come across that might someday be useful. Broken leather harnesses and bridles hung along the rear wall, the ends brushing the tops of huge, wooden barrels. Tools of the smithy's trade—heavy, iron hammers and long-handled tongs and sharp knives—shared wall space with the harnesses and bridles. Pitchforks and saw blades hung from the slatted loft above the stables, and the smithy's anvil stood off to the side of the door next to a trough of brackish water.

It all meant that any of a number of lethal weapons were within the smithy's easy reach.

The back door of the stable was closed, a heavy, wooden plank lowered into place to hold the doors closed. The smithy would have to let go of Vivian to lift the plank and open the door. He was backing up into a dead end.

"You have nowhere to go," Reggie said. "Let her go."

The smithy glanced over his shoulder and grunted. "Maybe I'll just take her with me. You boys wouldn't have any objections to that, now would you?"

Reggie locked eyes with Vivian, and in that moment he didn't see the frail-looking waif who sometimes dressed as a man on stage. He saw the girl who'd been on her own far sooner than a girl should be. He saw a girl who'd learned to take care of herself in a world full of men who wanted nothing more than to take advantage of her.

Vivian stomped down hard on the smithy's foot, then rammed her elbow into his belly.

The smithy yelled in surprise more than pain, but he must have loosened his grip on Vivian. She fell to the ground and rolled out of the way at the same time Cole fired.

Cole's shot hit the smithy in the left shoulder. The bullet staggered him, but didn't bring him down. He picked up a hammer from on top of the anvil, got a good grip on it, and with a bellow, charged Reggie.

Cole fired again, but this time his shot missed the smithy and ricocheted off a saw blade.

Reggie looked around frantically for something close enough to grab as a weapon, but then the smithy was on top of him. Reggie barely got his hands up in time to grab the smithy's wrist to keep the hammer from bashing into his skull, and then they were falling backward.

Reggie hit his head on something hard as he fell. His vision swam and grayed out.

He tried to stay focused on the need to keep the man's arm from swinging down and bringing the hammer with it, but it was so hard to think with the man's foul breath in his face and pain filling his head. He heard Cole's yell like it came from far away, too far away to answer.

Gravel crunched, a cloud of dust swirled around him as he fought with the smithy, and somewhere a horse neighed, high and frightened.

Then the fight seemed to go out of the smithy all at once. He collapsed in a heap on top of Reggie.

Reggie blinked to clear his eyes even as Cole pushed the smithy off him.

"Reggie!" Cole's worried face swam into focus above him. "Goddamn, are you hurt?"

Cole was holding his gun backwards, and Reggie realized he'd clubbed the smithy with the butt end of his revolver. Cole dropped the gun on the ground and, with gentle hands, cradled Reggie's head.

"I'm okay," Reggie managed to say, even though he wasn't sure if that was totally true. "How did you know..."

Cole smiled a worried smile. "I couldn't stay away. Figured you were up to something, and when I heard about your play, I had to see it. Thought I'd catch him here alone afterward, what with half the town down by the church, and do what I had to do to get him to leave me alone." Cole stroked Reggie's cheek. "Never thought he'd be dragging the two of you back here with him."

"Neither did we," Vivian said. She had picked herself up off the ground and stood behind Cole, brushing dirt off her dress. "So, this is the man we've done all this for?"

"This is Cole," Reggie said.

Vivian looked back and forth between the two of them. Reggie had never told her why they'd set a trap for the smithy, but he could tell by her expression that she'd figured it out. Or at least most of it. The smithy had never actually shown her Reggie's watch, so she had no reason to connect Cole with the stagecoach robbery. Maybe that was for the best.

The smithy grunted and snuffled. He was waking up.

Reggie scrambled to get away from the man. Cole kicked the heavy hammer away from the smithy's out-flung arm, retrieved his gun, and helped Reggie to his feet.

"Not over, you know," the smithy mumbled. His eyes opened. He tried to sit up, groaned, and grabbed at his shoulder. His shoulder was a mess, blood running down the front of his shirt and staining the ground beneath him, but Reggie could tell it wasn't a fatal wound. "I still got enough to go get that reward."

"You don't have anything," Reggie said. "If you did, you would have collected the reward long ago. What you have is my stolen property in your possession and an accusation you can't prove."

Cole looked startled, as if he just figured out exactly what Reggie had done.

"Don't need to prove it," the smithy said. "He shot me." The smithy grimaced as he finally succeeded in sitting up.

"And you attacked me," Vivian said.

A thin line of blood ran down her neck from where the smithy had cut her. Reggie felt guilty again for getting her involved.

"Half the town must have seen you drag me away," Vivian said. "Reggie and this nice man—Cole—they came to my rescue."

Her face looked fierce and terrible, as if it

wasn't just the smithy she was talking to, but someone else who had mistreated her badly.

"I don't know what you think you can accuse Cole of, but trust me, you don't want me accusing you of what you so clearly intended." Her expression changed, and she was once again the frail and waif-like girl who sometimes dressed as a boy on stage. "I can be very convincing."

Rage made the smithy's face turn red and ugly, but he sat on the filthy dirt floor of his stables and said nothing.

"Vivian, let's go." Reggie held out his hand. "We need to get ready for tonight."

The company had a late performance at the opera house. In two more days they'd be leaving Virginia City for the next stop on the company's tour. Reggie would need to talk to the director before then, but for now, all he wanted was to get as far away from the smithy as he could.

"I won't forget this," the smithy said to Reggie. "You got a secret too now, remember that."

Reggie could tell it was a hollow threat.

The smithy looked like a little bully whose favorite toy was broken.

Vivian spared the smithy one more pitying glance, then she took Reggie's hand and walked out of the stables, her head held high.

Cole joined them after a minute. Color was high on his cheekbones, and his eyes were a hard, icy blue.

"Cole?" Reggie risked a brief touch of his hand to Cole's as they walked. For just a moment their fingers entwined, and Cole squeezed his hand, then let go. "Are you all right?" Reggie asked.

Cole let out a deep breath. Reggie could almost see the tenseness go out of his shoulders.

"I will be now." He turned his head to look at Reggie, and the ice was gone from his gaze. "I will be now."

CHAPTER NINETEEN

"I'm going to miss you, you know." Vivian's eyes were watery. Reggie knew the tears were real, and he felt his own eyes burn. "The company won't be the same without you."

She hugged him then, a hard, unladylike hug that nearly crushed the air out of him.

Reggie bent his head and kissed her neck, right above the healing wound from where the smithy had cut her. He hoped the wound wouldn't leave a scar, but something told him Vivian wouldn't mind if it did.

The four actors had gathered one last time

in Reggie's dressing room. His one and only dressing room, at least for now.

Earlier that night Reggie had taken the stage for the last time as an actor for the San Francisco Shakespeare Company. The company would be leaving Virginia City in the morning. Reggie wouldn't be going with them. As much as he knew it would hurt to leave the company, it would have hurt more to leave Cole, and Reggie knew he couldn't have both.

Once Vivian let him go, Jeremiah held out his hand. Reggie reached out to shake it, but Jeremiah surprised him by pulling him into a hug as well.

"Don't know why you're leaving us," Jeremiah said. "Can't say I won't miss you, but I do wish you well."

Reggie looked over Jeremiah's shoulder at Vivian and Blanche. The two women shared a look, and Reggie realized Vivian had told Blanche that Reggie was leaving the company because he was in love. Reggie hoped Vivian had at least kept the details of his love life to herself.

When the hug was finished, Reggie turned

to Blanche. Instead of hugging him, she gave him a kiss on his cheek.

"Best of luck to you, Reggie," she said. "I hope if you're not going to act, that you give some thought to writing. The play you penned for us was marvelous."

Reggie thanked her even as he felt his cheeks flush.

The play had been adequate; it was the subject matter that made it interesting to write.

Reggie and the rest of the company had received a great deal of praise for the play, both from people who stopped them on the street and the children who sent them carefully printed notes. The parish priest made a point to stop by the opera house the evening after the benefit performance to tell Reggie how successful it had been and to thank him once again for his efforts on behalf of the families of the men lost in the mine.

It was the benefit to the families that made Reggie feel at all good about what had happened. He'd felt so guilty about putting Vivian in danger that he became over-protective to compensate, until Vivian finally told him that he'd have to stop or she might arrange a personal demonstration of how well she could defend herself against unwanted advances.

He realized now, with perfect hindsight, that his plan couldn't have worked the way he wanted it to. He supposed it had ended as best it could—in a draw, thanks in no small part to Vivian—but he worried that the smithy would still try to hurt Cole. It was one of the reasons he'd been able to talk Cole into leaving Virginia City.

Blanche leaned in closer to whisper in his ear. "I'm happy for you, Reggie," she said. "Everyone should find love, I do believe that."

Reggie grinned, he couldn't help it, even as he felt his face grow hotter. "Thank you," he murmured. "I hope you've found it as well."

It was an ill-kept secret that Blanche and Jeremiah did more than rehearse behind closed doors. Blanche looked the better for it, and Jeremiah seemed to be drinking less in between performances these days.

"I believe I have," she said.

Reggie could see Jeremiah looking vaguely worried. Reggie and Blanche were standing very close to each other and whispering things Jeremiah couldn't hear.

Unfortunately, Reggie couldn't tell Jeremiah that he had nothing to worry about. Vivian was the only one who knew Reggie was leaving Virginia City with Cole, heading east to start a new life together.

Reggie and Blanche stepped away from each other, much to Jeremiah's relief. Reggie finished saying goodbyes that were surprisingly painful, for all that it was his choice to leave the company, and then the actors left him alone in his dressing room.

He would miss this. He'd worked a long time to become a lead actor, but with any luck he would find another company that would have him. He and Cole planned to travel to New York City, and from there find passage on a ship headed to France. Reggie hoped that once in France he could find work again on stage, even though he would be living with Cole more openly there.

Reggie packed all his costumes carefully away. The last to go in the trunk was a cream-colored linen shirt he'd worn the first night the company had performed.

Had Cole been watching him even then? Reggie had never been with anyone who seemed so devoted to him. He wasn't entirely sure he deserved Cole's love, but he was certain he would do his best to be the man Cole thought he was.

Once the trunk was packed, Reggie left his dressing room. He wanted to stand on stage one last time before he went to his room at the hotel to collect his things. He and Cole would be leaving in the morning. Tonight they were staying at Cole's house for the last time.

So many last times.

Reggie felt a little melancholy standing alone on the darkened stage. It didn't seem the same without the other actors. Without an audience. Even the noise and smell of smoke and alcohol bleeding into the opera house from the saloon seemed subdued somehow.

Except maybe he did have an audience. Reggie thought he saw movement in the private box to the left of the stage, the box where Cole had hidden in the shadows to watch him.

"Cole," Reggie murmured, and his mouth

tilted up in a smile. Of course. Cole had come to see him on stage one last time, too.

Reggie took the back stairs to the box two at a time, heedless of the fact that the stairs were poorly lit and narrow. He wanted more than anything to kiss Cole in the shadows, maybe touch and be touched in this place that had come to mean so much to the both of them.

The door to the box stood ajar. Reggie pushed it open, expecting to see Cole smiling at him.

He wasn't expecting the blow that sent him to his knees.

"Thought I'd just give up and skulk away, I bet," the smithy said.

Chapter Twenty

Reggie shook his head, trying to clear it, but his ears were ringing from the impact of whatever the smithy'd hit him with.

"Come up here to find Cole, only you found me instead." The smithy's voice was thick with anger. "I don't disappear so easy. But you're gonna."

Reggie looked up in time to see the smithy swing at him again.

He managed to get an arm up to block the blow. The hardwood cane the smithy swung only struck him a glancing blow to the head, but his arm exploded in pain. He fell in between two of the heavy, wooden chairs in the box.

His arm was broken, Reggie was sure of it.

He needed a weapon, and he needed to get away from the smithy.

His eyes were adjusting to the dimness in the box, but it was still so hard to see. He scrambled around a chair, clutched at the back of another one with his good hand, all the time looking for something to use to defend himself. The chairs were too heavy for him to lift with only one arm.

The smithy sent one of the chairs crashing off the wall with another swing. His bandaged shoulder didn't seem to be hindering him.

"Go ahead and hide," the smithy said. "Don't make no difference to me how you die."

Reggie didn't intend to die here, not like this.

He pushed himself to his feet. He tucked his useless left arm in close to his body and grabbed the back of a chair with his right, keeping the chair between himself and the smithy.

Only the man wasn't coming after him anymore. He stood in the doorway to the box, a vicious smile on his face.

As Reggie watched, the smithy swung his cane again, only not at Reggie this time. His blow smashed the lantern fastened to the wall next to the door.

Reggie smelled the odor of lamp oil as it sprayed across the floor inside the door. He realized what the man intended to do even as the smithy struck a match and dropped it in the oil.

"No!"

Reggie's shout echoed off the walls along with the smithy's laughter.

Flames spread out across the floor from the spilled oil and licked up the side of the box, spreading quickly on the dry wooden wall.

The smithy smashed the lamp on the other wall, sending a fresh spray of oil into the fire, and the flames seemed to leap up to engulf both sides of the doorway.

The sudden heat from the fire drove Reggie back.

The fire separated him from the doorway. The only other way out was over the front of the box, but it was too high above the ground floor.

Reggie couldn't crawl over the edge of the box and try to climb down to lessen his fall, not with a broken arm.

"Reggie!"

He heard Cole's panicked shout from the narrow stairway beyond where the smithy stood.

The air was thick now with smoke. Reggie tried to shout his own warning, but he breathed in a lung full of smoke that turned his shout into a bout of coughing.

Cole's boot steps pounded up the stairs. Reggie saw the smithy turn, cane raised, and then the smoke and flames obstructed his view.

The two men fought and grappled with each other in silhouette, and then through the hissing and crackling fire, Reggie heard a heavy thud as something fell down the stairs.

Oh god... Cole!

He had to get out of there. If the smithy had knocked Cole down the stairs, Cole could be hurt. Dying.

Reggie wasn't about to let that happen, not when their life together was just starting.

The box had nothing he could use as a

weapon, but maybe he could use the heavy curtains at the front to keep the fire off him long enough to get to the stairs.

He yanked hard at the fabric, coughing and shouting his frustration as the curtains refused to give way. Each pull on the curtains jarred his broken arm, sending fresh jolts of pain through him.

Finally—*finally*—the fabric started to give way.

Reggie ripped it off the wall and draped it over himself as best he could. Before he could think about what he was doing, he ran for the door.

The heat and pain were incredible. Reggie could feel his skin tightening and burning even through the heavy drapes, and he smelled the fabric start to smoke.

A cry ripped from his throat as flames licked at his fingers, and then he was through the fire.

He dropped the drapes just as they exploded in flame.

Reggie stumbled down the first few steps, coughing and wheezing, his eyes watering, and then he saw the crumpled shapes at the bottom of the stairs.

He ran the rest of the way down, heedless of his broken arm and burned fingers and the fire rapidly spreading overhead. He heard distant shouts—the men in the saloon must have discovered the fire—and the even more distant ringing of the alarm.

None of that mattered. All he cared about was Cole.

The smithy and Cole had both fallen down the stairs.

The smithy was dead, his neck broken. His eyes were open, staring overhead at the conflagration he'd started.

Cole lay beneath him, not moving.

Reggie shoved the smithy off and crouched down over Cole. He felt along Cole's neck for a pulse.

In his haste he missed it, and for a heart-stopping moment he thought Cole had died in the fall, too.

Then Cole coughed and his eyes fluttered open.

Reggie choked out a sob. "We have to get

out of here," he said. "Can you stand? Are you hurt?"

Cole's eyes widened as he saw Reggie.

Much later he would tell Reggie that he'd thought Reggie was on fire. Reggie's clothes were smoking, his face was bright red, and his eyebrows had been singed off.

It had scared Cole enough that even though he didn't know how badly he'd been hurt in the fall, he'd gotten to his feet and pulled Reggie out of the stairway. He hadn't stopped until they were both outside, breathing blessedly clean night air.

Reggie grabbed Cole in a hug that made them both groan.

Blood was running down Cole's face from a gash in his head, and he held himself stiffly.

"Are you all right?" Reggie asked.

Cole clutched at Reggie and buried one hand in Reggie's singed hair. He sobbed against Reggie's neck. "Think I broken my damn shoulder," he said. "My head feels like I got kicked by a horse. And I've never been so glad to be alive, just to hold you and know we're both still here."

Reggie knew exactly how he felt.

Soon—too soon—they had to separate as men swarmed around the opera house, forming a bucket brigade. Someone wrapped a blanket around Reggie; someone else led Cole away.

"What happened? Reggie, what happened?"

Vivian stood in front of him, her eyes wide and frightened.

"The smithy," Reggie said.

A bout of coughing nearly doubled him over. Someone handed him a mug, and he drank down the ale without even tasting it.

"He started the fire. Trapped me. Cole, he..." Reggie looked around, tried to see Cole in the mass of people fighting the fire, but even with the flames shooting up high into the night, the smoke obscured his view. "Where is he?" Reggie dropped the mug, clutched his broken arm, and started to push his way through the crowd. "Cole!"

Vivian stopped him. "Ssshh, honey, he's fine. The doctor's looking at his shoulder, and then we need to get your burns and your arm looked at, too."

She steered him away from the crowd to

stand next to Blanche. She was here with Jeremiah, and Reggie saw the company's director standing a few feet away.

They were all watching the opera house burn, stricken looks on their faces.

All the costumes and props were still inside.

The bucket brigade tried its hardest, but it soon became apparent the opera house was a total loss. The alcohol in the saloon fed the flames, and fire engulfed the entire structure. The brigade stopped trying to save the opera house and instead worked on saving the buildings next to it.

Vivian and Jeremiah took Reggie to the doctor. They held him while the doctor set his arm and smeared ointment on his burns.

Afterward, Vivian took the doctor aside, and they exchanged a few whispered words.

The doctor glanced at Reggie, and his expression seemed to soften. He nodded, then came back over to Reggie.

"I hear thanks are in order," the doctor said. "From what this young lady says, it appears you and Cole captured our elusive bandit."

Reggie blinked at Vivian. She gave him a

subtle nod.

"He did have my pocket watch," Reggie said. "The bandit took it when he robbed our stage."

Both statements were true, just not the entire truth, but Reggie didn't feel guilty one wit for implicating the smithy as the bandit, not now.

The doctor grunted. "Seems like the two of you might be entitled to a substantial reward for your troubles. Might make your convalescence a little easier."

Reggie didn't care about the reward. "How is Cole?"

"Broken collarbone, cracked rib. A few burns here and there. He'll get better." The doctor peered at him. "So will you. You're a very lucky young man."

Reggie's arm throbbed, his fingers hurt even within their cocoon of ointment and bandages, and his face burned.

In the time he'd been in Virginia City he'd been robbed at gunpoint, beaten, and nearly burned alive.

He'd also become a professional actor,

written a play, and organized a performance for the benefit of widows and their children.

Most importantly, he had fallen in love.

Lucky? He most certainly was.

CHAPTER TWENTY-ONE

Reggie sat on a roan gelding near the summit of Mount Rose. The mountain rose to majestic heights above the Washoe valley. In the distance he could see the faint glimmering of a sky-blue mountain lake.

The air up here was cool, the sky brilliant. Reggie had never been on such a high mountain before in his life. The view was magnificent.

Next to him, Cole sat on his bay mare, smiling at Reggie's obvious joy.

"It's beautiful here," Reggie said.

They'd ridden up the steep slope of the

mountain, taking their time picking a path among ancient, towering pines and massive, granite boulders. The pines had stopped abruptly, and the ground leveled off into a high mountain meadow full of wildflowers.

"Thank you for bringing me to see it," Reggie said.

Cole reached out and took Reggie's hand, and held it gently.

Reggie squeezed back, grateful that he could. His burned fingers had healed, but the skin was scarred and he still couldn't bend his fingers without pain.

His eyebrows had grown back, and his broken arm had nearly healed. Cole's collarbone and rib had healed well enough to ride, although his collarbone pained him in the morning and late at night.

They hadn't left Virginia City as soon as they had planned. It took two weeks before either of them was up to riding on a horse.

They managed to meet frequently, with the help of the doctor, although meeting became difficult after Cummings grudgingly gave them the reward money.

He'd really had no choice.

The sheriff had found the burlap mask Reggie had hidden in the smithy's stables. Cole was questioned about his fight with the man at the opera house, but he was never suspected of being the masked bandit.

The smithy had been buried in the cemetery with a plain, wooden cross for a marker, and the search for the stagecoach bandit had been buried with him.

With Cole's blessing, Reggie had contacted the parish priest from St. Mary's in the Mountains about using the reward to set up a fund to support the families of men who died in the Orphir mine.

They'd kept only enough of the reward to buy a horse for Reggie and enough supplies to last for the first few weeks of their journey. The rest of the money had gone to do what Cole thought Cummings should have done all along. That, he'd said, was the height of irony.

They still planned to travel to New York City and then to Paris, but they'd decided to take their time.

Acting could wait. Reggie wanted this time

for himself and Cole. He knew how close he'd come to losing everything in the fire. Life didn't have that many second chances.

Reggie nudged his horse closer to Cole. "I have a marvelous idea," he said

Cole raised an eyebrow. "You do?"

"Yes." Reggie stroked the back of Cole's hand with his thumb. "I've always wanted to make love to you in a field of wildflowers. Think this one will do?"

Cole chuckled. "Won't get any complaints from me."

"I certainly hope not."

They kissed until the horses shifted beneath them and it was either stop kissing or tumble off their saddles.

They spread out blankets beneath the crystal blue sky. They touched and loved and laughed while the horses grazed nearby.

Afterward, they held hands while they talked about their pasts and what they hoped the future would bring.

This wasn't the life Reggie had expected to find when he came to Virginia City.

It was better.

He couldn't ask for anything more than that.

AUTHOR'S NOTE

The original Piper's Opera House in Virginia City was destroyed by fire in 1875. The owner, John Piper, rebuilt the opera house at the rear of a saloon he owned in another location.

The second opera house was also destroyed by fire in 1883.

Reggie and Cole had nothing to do with it.

ABOUT THE AUTHOR

Aaron Michaels is a romantic at heart. While he's not averse to writing the occasional hard-edged story, he prefers his characters to get at least a happy for now, if not happily ever after ending.

When he's not writing, Aaron watches way too much television and too many movies, which means his video game skills have pretty much fallen by the wayside.

For more information about Aaron, go to www.aaron-michaels.com.

www.ingramcontent.com/pod-product-compliance
Lightning Source LLC
Chambersburg PA
CBHW032011240626
47153CB00003B/1205